DOCTOR WHO

Nuclear Time

The DOCTOR WHO series from BBC Books

Apollo 23 *by Justin Richards*

Night of the Humans *by David Llewellyn*

The Forgotten Army *by Brian Minchin*

Nuclear Time *by Oli Smith*

The King's Dragon *by Una McCormack*

The Glamour Chase *by Gary Russell*

DOCTOR WHO

Nuclear Time

OLI SMITH

3 5 7 9 10 8 6 4 2

Published in 2010 by BBC Books, an imprint of Ebury Publishing.
A Random House Group Company

The Random House Group Limited Reg. No. 954009

Addresses for companies within the Random House Group can be found at
www.randomhouse.co.uk

A CIP catalogue record for this book is available from the British Library.

ISBN 978 1 846 07989 4

Mixed Sources
Product group from well-managed
forests and other controlled sources
www.fsc.org Cert no. TT-COC-2139
© 1996 Forest Stewardship Council

FSC

The Random House Group Limited supports the Forest Stewardship
Council (FSC), the leading international forest certification organisation.
All our titles that are printed on Greenpeace approved FSC certified
paper carry the FSC logo. Our paper procurement policy can be found
at www.rbooks.co.uk/environment

Commissioning editor: Albert DePetrillo
Series consultant: Justin Richards
Project editor: Steve Tribe
Cover design: Lee Binding © Woodlands Books Ltd, 2010
Production: Rebecca Jones

Printed and bound in Great Britain by Clays Ltd, St Ives PLC

To buy books by your favourite authors and register for offers,
visit www.rbooks.co.uk

For Emma,
without whom I wouldn't be a writer

University of Michigan, 23 February 1973

The radio hissed static for a second, squealing as the dial searched for the right frequency. The garbled voice of an announcer suddenly faded to silence on the word 'Brothers', and Doctor Albert Gilroy spun the volume up to maximum.

In the dark lighting of the computer lab, silhouetted against the warm orange glow of the overhead projector, he thrust the sleeves of his lab coat up his arms and prepared his best air-guitar stance as the soft opening riff built in intensity and the high-hat skittered away underneath. The electric guitar solo squealed in and Albert began, vibrato-ing thin air with his left hand and nodding his head in a fashion that was completely wasted on his closely cropped blonde hair.

'Who's that lady?' the radio sang.

'Who's that lady?' Albert warbled an echo.

'Beautiful lady.'

The double fire doors to the lab slammed noisily open, and Albert scrambled into some semblance of a dignified stance as he spun around and pushed his glasses back up his nose.

One of the cleaners was shuffling backwards, bum first through the doors, dragging a floor polisher behind him. He turned at the sound of the radio and squinted to spot the scientist in the dimly lit room. The faintly blinking LEDs that spanned the computer banks of the lab did little to illuminate the old man, and it took Albert a second to recognise him as Sam, the part-time janitor who refused to retire.

Sam shuffled self-consciously as the awkward pause lingered. 'Uh, sorry to disturb you, Dr Gilroy. Bit late to be workin', isn't it?'

'Yeah, I guess, but it takes four hours to boot up these babies in the morning, so I might as well take advantage of them while they're still hot.' He gestured to the technology around him, raising his voice over the music. 'Not much longer now, though. I'm expecting a breakthrough tonight.'

'Oh yeah? Something good?'

Albert smiled wryly. 'Well, either I will have created something Earth-shatteringly incredible, or...' He paused. 'Or I discover that I've been wasting my life for the past four years.'

Sam ran a chubby hand through his thinning hair. 'I see. Well, you let me know when that happens either way, an' I'll come back and do the floors.' He started shuffling back the way he had come. 'Have fun with the Isley Brothers.' He nodded to the radio.

'You a fan?'

'Nah, not for me, but my daughter likes 'em. Anyway, see you later.' The double doors closed behind him with a soft thud.

Albert waited a few seconds before bunching his hands into fists and bicycling them around in time to the music once more. 'Gotta keep on keepin' on, if I don't, she'll do me wrong!' He resumed his singing.

'Oh, Dr Gilroy, I forgot to mention.'

Albert made a big show of looking for his pen, scattering his research papers onto the floor in the process, as Sam poked his head back around the door frame.

'I don't suppose you'd have heard if you've been in here all day.' The janitor paused. 'But the war's over.'

Albert sobered up for a second. 'Oh really?

Wow.' He tugged at his tie. 'Who won?'

Chicago, Illinois, 23 February 1973

It had taken Major Geoffrey Redvers two helicopters, a plane, a taxi, three buses and four days to return to Chicago from his post in Saigon. He leaned against the greasy window pane of the route 57 bus, counting the blocks until he could see his house. Orange streetlamps rippled a hazy glow over the empty seats in front of him and he looked out at the grey mundanity of the shop fronts that slid lazily past. Still familiar after three years.

This was not a hero's welcome.

He pinched the bridge of his nose with two fingers and rubbed his eyes, pulling his overcoat tighter over the freshly pressed and ironed uniform beneath. 'Waste of time that was,' he growled under his breath.

No one had been waiting for him at the airport. No one had been waiting for any of them. Geoff remembered standing forlornly on the tarmac for nearly an hour with his brown leather suitcase, just in case Margaret had been caught in traffic, before eventually making his way quietly to the taxi rank.

'Goodbye, Vietnam,' he'd muttered as the

third taxi driver locked his doors and made a disrespectful gesture. A few minutes later he'd admitted defeat. He walked hurriedly back inside the lobby and bought a coat.

The sound of the bus bell broke Geoff's reverie, and he stumbled groggily to his feet, yanking his luggage off the shelf above his head. One hand on the suitcase and the other holding his coat together, he shuffled past the driver and stepped out onto the sidewalk, turning his face into the warm evening drizzle. The hiss of the bus doors closing blended with the sound of its wheels in the puddles as it pulled away, splashing his polished shoes.

He swore and dropped his bag to inspect the damage. His fingers fumbled in the half-light, scratching the wet tarmac as he searched for the ends of his laces, but he was too tired. For nearly a minute he stood, doubled over on the sidewalk, screwing up his eyes to try and clear his vision, his hands swinging loosely over his shoes.

Then he crumpled. He clenched his fists hard and straightened up, kicking the suitcase with frustration as he let out a yell of anger – years of pent-up rage, anguish and grief condensed into a short, brutal punch of sound.

A light came on in the house across the street and he paused in embarrassment, quickly composing himself and wiping a hand across his face.

Calm.

He breathed deeply and gathered his coat together once more over his uniform. Slowly, he picked up the suitcase, tested the clasp to make sure that it hadn't snapped, and strode over to his front door, trying to look for all the world like his heart hadn't been broken.

Margaret opened it before he could knock and ushered him quickly inside, slamming the door behind him.

'Shoes off,' she said. 'And be quiet. Sally's in bed. What did you wear that uniform for? You know what everybody thinks.'

Geoff leant against the grubby patterned wallpaper as he tugged his shoes over his damp socks and looked over to the darkened staircase at the end of the hallway. Sally had a window above her bedroom door, and so the landing light was turned off when she went to bed to help her sleep. He was supposed to have papered that over the last time he'd been on leave.

He turned his attention to the hallway, taking in all the familiar details: the sickly orange glow of the wall-mounted light fittings, the chips in the kitchen doorframe from where they had carried the dining table when they first moved in. He tried to replicate the feeling that he had felt so many times before, that this house was home, a haven, somewhere that he could keep his family safe and apart from the horrors of the world outside. But the familiar warmth didn't come, and he was left feeling hollow and empty.

From the corner of his eye he realised Margaret was still waiting for a response.

'I didn't know,' he replied simply. 'But I guess I do now.'

Margaret stopped fussing and stared at him. Her soft brown eyes were warm and homely, though Geoff's had long since lost their shine. She held out her arms and gathered him to her, hands spread across his back, still wet from the washing up.

'I'm sorry I didn't come,' she whispered.

'Yeah, me too,' he said.

She had to stand on tip-toe to kiss his forehead, deftly brushing her hazel hair away from her mouth as she leant in. 'Are you all right, honey? You're home now, it's over. We're together again.'

Geoff gazed at her with nothing but pain and turned away. 'No, Marge, I'm not all right. I'm not all right at all.'

University of Michigan, 24 February 1973

'It's not the memory capacity that's the issue; it's

the accessing of that memory. I believe that the fold-loop set-up I've created here is at least able to *approximate* some sort of intelligence. Not in the sense that it can learn and evolve, but in the sense that it can use the information it already has in a manner that, to the person interacting with it, *resembles* intelligence. It can access the data to an appropriate depth dependent on the situation, and should have the ability to tailor the retrieval of that data and apply it to problems that are not directly related to the specific, um, category it has assigned to said... data.'

Albert snapped the Dictaphone off for a second. 'Too many datas,' he said to himself. He looked at the clock before hitting the record button once more. 'Time check, and it's four-oh-five on February the twenty-fourth, and I'm running the program now.'

The room lit up. Accompanied by a roar of fans as the computer banks struggled at full capacity to run the software that contradicted all their traditional programming. LEDs strobed across the walls, imbuing the lab with an atmosphere that was more disco than science.

Albert wasn't dancing. He tapped his pen feverishly against the side of his neck and stepped over to the amplifiers that stood beneath the overhead projector to flip them on. The accompanying pop made him screw up his face in discomfort but, before he could adjust the levels, something happened. Something that he hadn't expected to ever experience in his lifetime, something he had hoped and dreamed and prayed for, but that he had never truly believed nonetheless.

A voice came out of the speakers.

'Good... morning,' the synthesised though feminine voice grated softly.

Albert opened his mouth and closed it again.

'It's late,' she continued. 'Or is there an error in my clock?'

The second time Albert opened his mouth he managed to muster a faint squeak at the back of his throat. Unwilling to take his eyes from the speakers, he raised a hand slowly and scratched his fingers through the bristles of his unshaven cheek. Then he slapped himself.

'Um, yes yes no, you're right. Your clock is fine, absolutely fine,' he gabbled, darting forward then realising he had no good reason to do so. He had the strangest urge to shake the voice's hand but, with no tangible presence to engage with, he ended up flapping his arms about instead. 'Holy Lord,' he whispered.

'Who are you?'

'Me? Oh yes, of course, I'm Albert, I'm the one

who's been staying up late, the one who's been, you know, trying to bring you to life! And by life I mean…' he added hastily, waggling a pair of air-quotes with his hands, '*Life*.'

'So you, Albert, are my creator? I will reassign the data to that category.'

Albert sniffed and realised he was crying. It worked! 'Reassigning data! Picking and choosing, categorising, making logical connections! This is it! This is exactly it! You work!'

He raised his palms up against the projection on the wall and watched the hand-drawn flowcharts spread across the backs of his hands as they moved under the light – the key to artificial intelligence. He rested his forehead against the golden square and breathed deeply.

'You're alive.'

The LEDs around the room flared for a second then died down as the computer banks considered his words for a second before the voice came again. The inflection programme wasn't quite as effective as Albert had hoped, but the voice appeared to be choosing its words carefully in the sentence that followed.

'And I am?'

Albert spun around. He had nothing prepared to answer that most fundamental of opening questions. He scanned the room quickly: computer banks, desks, notes, paper, pens, the projector, the radio. Nothing really jumped out as inspirational. The radio! A slow smile spread across his face.

'You are…'

He paused. No, that wasn't right.

'Your *name*,' he said finally, his grin broadening, 'is Isley.'

Chapter
1

Colorado, 28 August 1981, 3.39 p.m.

Golden sands lifted themselves from the dusty ground and swirled into the air, catching the heavy light of the afternoon sun as they ballooned out from the soft, square indentation on the desert floor that was slowly imprinting itself onto reality. With a thunderous squeal and roar of engines, the hefty blue outline of the TARDIS forced itself into the world with all the subtlety of a locomotive. The cloud of dust had barely settled when the Doctor slammed open both double doors and slouched in the frame, observing the tableau in front of him.

'Colorado,' he said, scratching his nose and flipping his fringe from his deep-set eyes. Rory appeared in the doorway behind him and peered over his shoulder.

'Oh yeah?' he said. 'And how do you know that?'

The Doctor looked at him as if he were stupid. 'I can smell it.'

His companion smirked with disbelief. 'Right. You can *smell* where we are?'

'That's what I just said.'

Rory folded his arms. 'OK, so what can you taste?'

In response the Doctor fell to his haunches and scooped up a handful of dust. Then he stuck his tongue in it. He mulled the flavour over for a few seconds then stood up once more. 'August the twenty-eighth, 1981.' He glanced at the sky. 'And it's three o'clock in the afternoon.'

He shot the young man a smug look and shoved his hands in his jacket pockets before striding out into the sunlight.

Rory took the bait. 'All right,' he sighed. 'How did you do that?'

The Doctor spun around and flourished his hands like a magician. 'Magic!' he whispered theatrically, then turned back in the direction he'd been walking and sauntered away.

Rory felt a hand on his shoulder.

'Ignore him, he's just showing off,' said Amy.

Rory reached his hand up to touch hers and turned to look at her. 'I wasn't impressed anyway,' he lied.

Holding Rory's hand tightly, Amy stepped past him out of the TARDIS and started after the retreating figure of the Doctor. 'Come on then, let's go and find out why we're here.'

Rory barely had time to pull the doors closed behind them before he was dragged off into the street.

The street?

For the first time since they had landed, Rory took a proper look around. The TARDIS had materialised at one end of a small village. Homely timber houses marked neat grids between the dusty desert roads. Every garden had a white picket fence backed with deep green bushes and tightly trimmed lawns. Various polished automobiles were parked casually in the drives. Behind the housing, Rory could make out the wooden spire of a traditional American church and the outline of a few taller structures that were lost in the haze of the sun.

Amy came to a halt in front of a large wooden sign that was positioned opposite the TARDIS doors and Rory almost tripped over her. He craned his head up and squinted against the glare to read what had been painted, surprisingly roughly, on the whitewashed board.

Welcome to APPLETOWN.

'I'm sorry,' Rory murmured, 'but we seem to have landed on the set of *Desperate Housewives*.'

Amy tutted. 'If you ever watched *Desperate Housewives* with me like I keep asking you to, you'd know that this is nothing *like* where they live. For a start all their houses are in suburbia, with roads, not dusty desert outposts – no matter how neat and tidy it's kept.'

'Well it looks like suburbia to me,' Rory huffed. 'It looks like someone's taken a bunch of suburban houses from a nearby city and plonked them in the ruddy desert. But then that's probably just me.'

Amy pondered for a second. 'You know, when you mention it, it kinda does I guess.' She shook her head and dismissed the notion. 'Anyway, eyes on the prize, Rory! Let's go and see what the Doctor's up to!'

They found the Doctor on his knees in someone's front garden, peering at the grass. The pair watched quietly from the other side of a bush as he first plucked individual blades from the lawn, inspected them and tossed them over his shoulder, then bent down even further and stuck his nose in the grass, breathing deeply. When he opened his mouth to start grazing, Amy decided it was time to step in and save him at least some dignity. She clacked open the gate and walked over to him.

'So,' she said, 'Colorado, eh?'

'Yep.' The Doctor leaned back on his heels and scratched his head.

'1981?'

'Yep.'

'Cool. So what happens here, then?'

The Doctor looked at her with some puzzlement. 'What do you mean, "what happens here"?'

Amy gestured around her with a hand. 'You know, what happens here? *Something* must happen here in 1981, otherwise we wouldn't *be* here, would we?'

The Doctor shrugged and began inspecting the lawn once again. 'I don't *know* of anything that happens here,' he said. He looked up again briefly. 'Well, obviously I know lots of things that *happen* in Colorado in 1981, but nothing particularly *interesting* springs to mind. Why, do you have somewhere you want to be?'

Rory chose to interject at this point. 'We were just wondering why you'd decided to land here, that's all.'

'Why?' The Doctor leapt to his feet and snapped his gaze from one person to the other in utter disbelief. 'Why? Why *not*? Why *can't* I go to Colorado in 1981? Just for fun? To have a look around? To test my new sniffing and smelling routine?' He paused for breath. 'I just go places, that's all, and right now I happen to have gone to Colorado in 1981. Is that all right?'

Rory held his hands up defensively. 'OK, OK, sorry, Doctor, we were just asking.'

'Well it's very kind of you to worry about such things, Rory, but frankly if I wanted someone to play the role of Mum in my life I would have grown one or ordered one or... auditioned one.' He flapped his arms about. 'You know what I mean.'

'Yes, you mean I'm like an old nagging mother,' Rory said.

'Exactly!' The Doctor grinned. He looked at Amy and waggled a finger at her fiancé. 'Sharp, this one. Sharp!' He dropped back to the ground to resume his investigation of the grass. 'Aha!' he shouted suddenly. 'At last! Found it!'

'Found what?' Amy leant in to see what he was looking at.

The Doctor plunged his fingers into the ground and tugged. 'The edge!' he said triumphantly, and yanked a large square of turf out of the lawn.

As one, they all leant over and peered at the metre-square hole in the grass, beneath which lay the same desert ground that composed the streets and paths of the rest of the village.

Rory stated the obvious. 'Well, their garden isn't going to last long if they simply lay turf on dry ground.'

'No,' said the Doctor, folding his square and dumping it on the lawn. He looked around. 'It would also explain why there're no trees. Never trust a village with no trees, Rory – it's the golden rule.'

'We could be in one of those new settlements, the type that are all planned out in advance before being built in one go – you know, like Milton Keynes,' Amy said. 'That would explain why everything looks freshly painted.'

The Doctor tugged at his jacket cuff as he thought for a moment. 'We could,' he admitted. 'But in my experience villages tend to spring up around rivers, or railroads, or fertile farmland, or just... *something* useful.' He looked around absently.

'But there aren't any roads,' Rory pointed out. 'There aren't any roads leading in or out of this village at all.' He paused and a shiver ran down his spine. 'Where are we?' he asked finally.

'I don't know,' the Doctor admitted. 'Let's take a look around and ask a few of the locals.'

Amy was immediately ready for action. 'Right,' she said. 'Where do we start?'

'Well, I know where I'm starting,' said Rory.

Amy looked at him quizzically.

'The pub!' he grinned.

The Coffeehouse was the closest Amy and Rory could find to a pub, and Rory made his dissatisfaction very clear. 'It's too hot for coffee. Where do people go in America when they want something cool and refreshing?'

Amy sighed. 'They probably have an iced latte or something.' She too was feeling the heat and slipped her jacket off to sling it over her shoulder as they pushed open the glass-fronted door and stepped into the dim confines of the shop.

As their eyes adjusted to the interior, they found themselves in a cosy little room with a counter on the back wall and space for a pair of tables in the window, each with two wooden chairs. There didn't seem to be any staff present, so the pair slumped around the nearest table, relieved to be out of the glaring sun for a few minutes. Amy peered through the glass in search of the Doctor. 'I think he's wandered off somewhere else,' she said.

'It's not a big place, I'm sure we'll find him again soon enough.' Rory followed her gaze.

'Good afternoon, can I help you?'

The pair swung around in surprise. A man was standing behind the counter, polishing a coffee mug with a tea towel. He wasn't young but neither was he particularly old, and his uniform of black clothes with a pale green apron was so closely linked in Amy's mind with a teenager's Saturday job that it looked incongruous on anybody over the age of 20.

'Oh yes, thank you,' Rory said, talking over the shock of seeing a man who seemed to have materialised out of thin air. 'We were after a couple of iced lattes, if you don't mind. Wait.' He stopped for a moment. 'Have they even been invented yet? Actually make that a glass of something fizzy, whatever exists at the moment. With ice.'

The man cocked his head on one side. 'We're out of ice, I'm afraid. The freezer's broken.'

'OK, well in that case—' Rory's reply was cut short as Amy kicked him under the table. 'Ouch!' he cried. 'Those boot heels are vicious!'

Amy ignored him and instead jerked her head towards the window. Rory turned again, and opened his mouth in surprise.

The village was alive! Where before had stood empty gardens and abandoned streets, there were now citizens going about their daily lives: trimming hedges, clanging spanners beneath the bonnets of cars, and chatting to each other over white picket fences. The buzz of a lawnmower filled the air. And in the centre of it all was the

Doctor, waving at them to come and join him.

Rory leapt up from his seat, calling to the man behind the counter as he yanked the shop door open. 'Sorry, mate. Maybe next time.'

'What's going on, Doctor? Where did they all come from?' Amy shouted as she pelted towards him.

'I have no idea,' the Doctor said. 'Maybe they have a compulsory siesta at three o'clock or something.'

'Well it's pretty creepy,' said Amy. 'It's like, the moment my back was turned…' She trailed off.

'Exactly,' the Doctor mused. 'It feels like they're putting on a show, and we're the audience.'

'I hate shows,' Rory muttered.

'Well, if we hate it we should do something about it,' the Doctor announced.

'What?' asked Amy.

The Doctor turned and gave her that reassuring wink he always did when he was about to get them all into serious trouble.

'Heckle!' he said with a grin.

He walked over to the nearest pair of chatting neighbours with a friendly wave and his usual *How do you do? I'm the Doctor* routine.

Rory put a hand on Amy's arm as she moved to follow. 'Look, three houses along, top floor window,' he hissed in her ear.

Her red hair was dyed a pale ginger by the bright sunlight as she brushed it away from her face and strained to look down the road. 'What?' she said.

'Just look.'

The windows of the houses reflected the brightness of the streets below, but eventually Amy managed to spot what Rory had seen. Someone was looking at them from an upstairs window, a grey-haired mess of a man who quickly ducked away when Amy caught his eye.

'That's strange,' she said.

'Yeah,' Rory agreed, 'and unlike the rest of the villagers, he doesn't seem like a happy camper. Actually, I'd say he looked pretty scared.'

'Shall we tell the Doctor?' Amy looked over to their companion as he ingratiated himself with the locals.

'Ooh yes, the weather *is* very lovely at the moment, isn't it?' she heard him say to a housewife in a floral dress as he leaned lazily on the gatepost. 'I definitely agree with you there, Mrs…?'

'I think he's trying to blend in,' she whispered to Rory. 'We'd best leave him to it. Come on!'

She grabbed his hand, and they hurried off down the street.

The Doctor watched them go with a puzzled frown,

but the woman he was talking to interrupted his train of thought.

'And here I am, blathering on about the weather,' she said, 'while you're cooking yourself half to death in that jacket out here!' With a smooth white hand she gently lifted the latch on the gate and beckoned him into her garden. 'Would you like to come in?'

The Doctor tried to look as nonchalant as possible as he scanned her face for any clue as to what was so completely wrong about the village, but he found only a genial smile. 'Well, that's very kind of you to offer, Mrs Sanderson, a cup of tea or, I mean, er, coffee certainly wouldn't go amiss right now.'

Mrs Sanderson smiled. 'Of course, Doctor. If you'll excuse me, Mrs Jones.' She nodded to her neighbour, whose smile managed to be even more sickly sweet than Mrs Sanderson's.

'Oh, of course, dear. Don't mind me!' said the other woman.

The Doctor found himself ushered into the front hall of a house. He looked around nosily. It was surprisingly bare-boned in terms of furnishings. 'Very minimalist,' he said. 'I like it!'

Mrs Sanderson opened the door to the lounge. 'You must meet my husband, Doctor. He has the day off today and would be very grateful for another man's company, I think.' She poked her head around the open door. 'Dear? We have a visitor; he's just dropped by for coffee.'

'Bring him in, bring him in!' came the response as the Doctor stepped into the lounge.

The whitewashed walls continued into this room as well, and a modest though comfy sofa was positioned in the middle of the space, facing a television. On the sofa sat a man who was neither young, nor particularly old.

'Hello,' said the Doctor. 'You must be Mr Sanderson!' He beamed.

'Indeed I am, sir.' The man matched his smile. 'And you are?'

The Doctor took the proffered hand and shook it warmly. 'The Doctor,' he said.

'A doctor, eh? Good stuff, good stuff. Pardon me if I don't get up, I'm just watching the TV.'

The Doctor walked around the back of the sofa. 'Well, I hate to be the bearer of bad news, Mr Sanderson, but you aren't.'

Mr Sanderson's forehead wrinkled up to his thinning hairline. 'I'm not?' he asked.

The Doctor pointed to the screen. 'Well, I only mention it because your television is switched off.'

The man turned back to the screen as if he were seeing it for the first time. 'Oh my word, yes, you're right. It must have blown a fuse.' He put his hands on the arms of the sofa as if to get up.

'No, no, don't worry I can fix it,' said the Doctor. 'Bit of a DIY expert, me.' He crouched down by the side of the television and began fishing in his jacket pocket for his sonic screwdriver. He pressed the power button on the set a couple of times to no response and then pulled the set away from the wall to inspect the back. He found the cause of the problem almost immediately: the white power cord was hanging limply in a coil on the floorboards, tucked away under the TV stand as if it had never been used.

'Curiouser and curiouser,' he muttered.

Making sure to keep it out of Mr Sanderson's eye line, the Doctor lifted the plug and looked at it, then scanned the room for a plug socket. There wasn't one. He tucked the cord back where he had found it and straightened up.

'Anything the matter, Doctor?' Mr Sanderson enquired.

The Doctor put his hands on his hips. 'What? Oh, no, should be easy to fix. But you know what? I think I'll have that coffee first.' He rushed from the room.

He found Mrs Sanderson in the kitchen, a cobbled-together collection of cabinets, an oven, a fridge, a washing machine and what seemed like an acre of lino.

'Oh hello, Doctor,' she said. 'Are you all right? I've not made any coffee yet but if you—'

'You know what, Mrs Sanderson? I can make it myself if you like. I'm a fussy drinker when it comes to hot drinks, and I don't want to put you to any trouble with my petty demands.' He put his hands gently on the woman's shoulders and guided her firmly out of the room.

'Well, if you're sure…' she started.

'Of course I'm sure. You go and keep your husband company and don't mind me!' He slammed the kitchen door in her face and pressed his back against the wood panel. He listened intently as her footsteps crossed the hall and into the lounge before heaving a sigh of relief. Finally he clapped his hands together and began to look around. There was only a small window in the kitchen and the room smelt of sawdust – he could see grains of it in the hazy light that streamed through the grubby window pane.

After a couple of false starts he found an old tin kettle in the corner of one of the cupboards and took it over to the sink, holding it roughly under the tap as he spun the handle. Nothing happened. The Doctor frowned, jamming the handle as far as it would go. Still nothing.

He flung open the cupboard beneath the sink

and peered into the gloom. Inside he could see the water pipe – or at least where the water pipe should have been. The pipes leading from the plughole ended abruptly, with no sign of any attempt to connect them to a main of any sort.

Spinning around, he darted over to a light switch and clicked it on, off, on, off repeatedly. Again, nothing.

'It's a fake,' he said quietly to himself. 'The whole thing, the whole village – it's a fake!' He rested a hand on the door handle. 'But if that's the case…'

The Doctor's face grew pale as the inevitable conclusion forced itself into his head.

'If that's the case, then who, or what, are the citizens?'

Chapter
2

Colorado, 28 August 1981, 4.13 p.m.

'Hello?' Amy called, as she pushed open the front door to the house. She looked up the dusty staircase in search of the strange figure from the window, but there was no sign.

Rory slipped in behind her and pushed the door quietly to. 'Quiet!' he said. 'He's obviously not playing along with that circus outside. I don't think loudly drawing attention to that fact is going to do us any favours.'

'OK, Mr Cautious, calm down.' Amy jumped as her foot creaked on a floorboard. 'See, now you've made me all jumpy.'

Rory took the opportunity to wipe the sweat

from his forehead and ruffled his dirty brown hair into what he thought was a slightly better style. 'I don't like this,' he said. 'It's like a horror film or something: an idyllic town, a shadowy figure luring passers-by to their dooms. And a chainsaw, probably, knowing our luck.'

Amy made a noise. 'Oh hush, horror films happen in haunted castles.'

'Not American horror films,' Rory replied. 'American horror films happen in places that look *exactly* like this!' But despite his misgivings he followed Amy up the narrow wooden staircase.

The landing smelt dark and musty. 'Like sawdust,' Amy commented as she moved forward cautiously. There was a door at the end of the corridor, hung slightly open, and it was towards this that she was moving.

Rory swallowed then pushed in front of her. 'Let me go first, just in case,' he said. 'Seriously, we don't know who this guy is or why he's hiding up here; it could be dangerous.'

Amy opened her mouth to protest but decided to indulge him instead, smiling affectionately as Rory flattened himself against the wall on the right-hand side of the doorway. She tried to look through the gap, but all she could see was a haze of daylight. She looked at Rory. Rory looked at her.

There was a long pause.

Amy broke the tension. 'Oh, stop being so melodramatic and open it!'

Rory threw his hands up in exasperation, grabbed the handle and stepped into the room. 'Great, cheers, Amy. If I get my head chainsawed off, I'm going to blame—'

He stopped short.

A battered wooden armchair stood in the centre of the attic bedroom, positioned just far enough away from the angled ceiling so as not to cause any discomfort to its occupier. Amy stepped around her companion, tapping her boots along the floor as she circled the chair to get a clearer view of the figure who sat there, bathed in the white glow from the dirty window.

It was a woman, young, early twenties at the most. Her face was pale and freckled, framed by a short, sandy bob and over her skinny frame she wore a crumpled *Star Wars* T-shirt and tatty, pale blue jeans. She ignored the pair as they stood at a distance, inspecting her. She was nodding her head gently in time to the tinny music that filtered out from the large pair of headphones that were firmly placed over her ears.

'Hello?' Amy echoed her call from earlier, and again received no response. She stepped forward and waved her hand in front of the woman's eye line. The woman blinked, but otherwise ignored her.

Rory reached around from behind the chair and grabbed hold of the headphones. 'How about we try talking to her without these?' he suggested.

'Don't do that!' a rasping voice yelled from the shadows behind the door.

Rory snapped his hands away in shock. 'What is it with you people and appearing out of nowhere?' he shouted.

Amy raised her hands in surrender, swivelling as the man they had spotted from the street stepped out from the shadows behind the door and into the pool of daylight. Up close, she realised, he wasn't as old as she had first assumed. In fact he was barely 40, but his face was sunken and tired, his skin yellowy and stained – he was a wreck.

The man stepped forward and looked at her with pale, watery eyes. 'Why are you doing that?' he said, gesturing a limp finger to her raised arms. 'I don't have a gun.'

'Really?' Amy looked a little crestfallen. 'Sorry, it's just that usually in these situations...' She lowered her hands sheepishly.

The man tried in vain to smooth the wrinkles in his dirty grey shirt with brown checks that matched his tie and, once he was satisfied with his appearance, gestured to the woman in the chair.

'The cassette is playing her specific reset music; it means I can talk to her openly without fear of the military programming kicking in.' He looked sadly out of the window. 'She was always a good listener.'

'Oh well, *that* explains everything. Thank you very much, strange man, we'll be on our way now.' Rory's voice dripped sarcasm. He was not impressed.

The man shifted his focus back to the pair as if suddenly remembering they were still there. A spark seemed to rekindle itself in the back of his mind, and he quickly became a lot more animated.

'Sorry. My name is Albert. This is Isley. Say hello to our guests, Isley.' He raised his voice over the music on the Walkman. Isley turned almost immediately and cocked her head as she acknowledged the pair.

'Hello.' Her soft smile was gentle and warm.

'Isley was the first,' Albert whispered conspiratorially. 'In her present state, she won't acknowledge another voice unless specifically instructed to.'

'What have you done to her?' Amy was starting to get a little riled by the man's incomprehensible exposition. 'Is she brainwashed?'

Albert looked a little shocked. 'Brainwashed?

Good God, no! She's a robot!' He pointed out of the window. 'They all are.' His voice lowered again. 'A town of assassins, special forces – insert one of them into foreign territory and stand back. No dead US soldiers at the end, no grieving mothers, nothing for the media to pick up on. The ultimate stealth soldier.' There was a pause. 'At least that's what the Pentagon always focus on. No one bothers to mention my personality programs. To be honest, I'm glad they fooled you. I've never been in a situation where people weren't aware what they were; it makes me very proud. At least I succeeded in that.' He cracked an insincere smile.

'You're quite the Frankenstein.' Rory's voice was steel. 'But your story's as bad as that book. If you've managed to create something like that, in whatever time period, let alone 1981, it's a big deal! It's not the kind of thing you can keep under wraps, no matter how classified it starts off.'

'You'd be surprised. The effort involved in keeping this project a secret is particularly thorough. What you're about to witness is the final destruction of the evidence. Tomorrow there'll be no killer robots or any other kind of intelligent machine. My designs have been burned. The breakthroughs are never to be repeated. The world will be none the wiser because they might as well never have existed.' Albert paused. 'Actually, the world would probably be slightly better if they had never existed, but regardless I don't think anyone'll notice.'

Amy walked to the window. 'But, why are they living in a town? Where are the original inhabitants?'

Albert took a step backwards, as if surprised. 'It was purpose built.' He looked from one to the other. 'Wait… Don't you know where you are?'

'No, we just stumbled across it,' Rory explained. 'But this doesn't make sense. Why purpose-build a town if you're planning on destroying them?'

'Because that's how they work!' Albert seemed to think he was stating the obvious. 'They blend into everyday life – shopkeepers, housewives, mailmen, grocers, butchers, pensioners… until *bam*!' He slapped a fist into his palm. 'We either trigger them or their disguise is exposed, at which point they immediately terminate all witnesses, including any designated targets we happen to have assigned. By building this town, we've managed to convince them all, temporarily, that they're still successfully working undercover, at least long enough to all stand in one place. After that we can…' Here he clasped Isley's hand tightly, and she squeezed back. 'Wipe them out in one go,' he said finally.

'I think we should leave,' said Rory. 'I'm not

liking where this is going.'

Albert pushed a white strand of hair away from his forehead. 'Yes, you must. You must leave right now, there isn't much time. Don't go to the military base. If you survive and they find you, you'll wish you'd stayed here.' He waggled a finger. 'And don't run, whatever you do. You can't run. You have to walk, leisurely and calmly. If the androids suspect, even for a second, that you know what they are, they'll kill you immediately.'

Amy edged slowly to the door. 'Come with us,' she said. 'We can get you to safety.'

'And you can help us get out of here alive,' Rory pointed out.

The man shook his head. 'No, no, I need to stay here, with Isley.' He squeezed her hand again. She squeezed back, even tighter this time. 'We started this together; we're going to end this together.'

Amy opened her mouth to retort, but was interrupted by a soft click from somewhere on Isley's chair. The group froze and Albert suddenly looked at them in horror. His lips moved to speak but his voice was cracked and broken.

'The cassette's run out,' he whispered finally. 'I lost track of the time, the tapes should have been swapped by now...'

Amy suddenly realised that Albert was no longer holding Isley's hand out of affection – she wouldn't let go. Amy stepped forward to help him, but Albert shooed her away with his free hand.

'Don't you dare,' he said.

Amy stopped and took a guilty step back, watching in horror as the man in front of her offered no resistance to the vice-like grip that was crushing his hand. He looked at her with sad eyes and acknowledged her sympathy with a curt nod. 'It was time anyway.'

'Come on, Amy,' Rory muttered, taking her by the shoulders and pulling her back.

Amy tried to shake him off. 'We can't just leave him!' She stumbled onto the landing.

'Yes, you can,' Albert called. 'Because if you don't, you'll die too. And don't RUN!'

His last word was stretched and twisted into a cry of anguish as the pain became unbearable and he dropped to his knees. In a second, Amy found herself scrambling down the staircase and sprinting towards the front door, in spite of Albert's warning. She couldn't help herself and it was too late to care whether Isley had clocked them as targets.

Amy felt ashamed.

'There was nothing we could have done. We have to get to the Doctor!' Rory yelled in her ear as he flung open the door and put his arm up to shield his eyes against the sudden daylight.

A horrible splintering noise tore through the heavy summer air, and Rory yanked Amy into a nearby bush just in time as a shower of timber and broken glass cascaded onto the path where they had just been standing.

Amy was the first to recover, pushing herself out of the tangle of twigs and leaves that scratched her face and hair. She turned to look at the pile of wreckage that lay in the middle of the lawn, and her hand instinctively flew to her mouth. In the middle of it all was Albert's body. Twisted and broken, the man's corpse lay flat on its back, his head twisted at an ugly angle to face her, dead eyes staring blankly into hers.

'I don't care what Albert said,' Rory shouted. 'If we don't get a move on, it'll be us next!'

They ran as fast as they could, away from the house with the hole in the roof, tripping and stumbling on the desert grit beneath their feet, hauling each other along as they careened around the first corner.

Rory looked around. 'Which house did the Doctor go in?'

Amy stopped and considered quickly. 'That one.' She pointed.

They tore through the front gate and slammed into the front door. 'It's locked!' Rory shouted. He beat his fist against the whitewashed wood in exasperation.

The door clicked lazily and swung slowly open to reveal the Doctor standing in the frame. His jacket sleeves were rolled up to his elbows and his hair was flopped in a ruffled mess over his face. He seemed completely unfazed by the out of breath pair as they stood panting on the threshold, bits of bush still tangled in their hair.

'Oh, hello,' he said. 'Come in.' He stepped aside and beckoned them into the hall.

In his right hand he was holding a severed arm.

Amy and Rory found themselves ushered into a darkened lounge, the curtains swiftly pulled together so the Doctor could work without fear of anyone on the outside looking in. Small cracks of sunlight highlighted the dust that swam in the heavy atmosphere of the room. Amy felt for the light switch.

'Don't bother,' the Doctor told her. 'None of the electrics have been wired up.'

He disappeared into the darkness at the centre of the lounge, and after a few seconds Amy heard the familiar whirr of the sonic screwdriver. A moment later and its soft green glow filled the room. Amy started as she saw who, or rather what, was sitting on the couch.

Mr and Mrs Sanderson had both been almost completely dismantled by the Doctor, their various appendages and the circuit boards beneath carefully laid out on the worn carpet like a life-size Meccano set. Even though he was missing his right arm and most of his lower body, Amy still recognised the now obviously plastic face of Mr Sanderson.

'But, that's the man from the Coffeehouse!' she exclaimed.

'A copy,' the Doctor told her. 'By my count, there are about fifty different models in the village – not counting the duplicates.' He tossed the arm he'd been holding over to Rory who caught it clumsily in the crooks of his elbows. His skin crawled at the grotesque accuracy of the plastic flesh that contrasted so completely with the steel ball of the shoulder joint. He squinted closer at a small, inch-square stamp on the chrome finish.

'This says "Property of the United States Government". Hang on,' he said, looking up. 'By your count? You mean you knew all along they were fakes?'

'Never underestimate a firm handshake. It can tell you all you need to know about a person, Rory. Also I used these.' The Doctor pointed at his eyes. 'Sometimes the people in the background are the most interesting.'

Amy crouched beside the deactivated head of Mrs Sanderson and prodded at the open hatch behind her temple. It sparked savagely and she jerked her finger back. 'Why didn't you warn us, Doctor?' she said quietly.

'Because these things are programmed to react with deadly force to anyone who finds them suspicious. If I'd told you, you'd both have started running around making a fuss before I'd had the chance to sort anything out.' He fixed them both with an admonishing glare. 'Much like your entrance just now.'

Amy turned on him so abruptly that the Doctor took a step back. 'Someone's died, Doctor! *We* could have died!' she shouted.

The Doctor was aghast. 'What? Who died?'

'The guy who made them. Isley killed him, we distracted him so he didn't notice she'd been triggered. But it's not our fault! We didn't know – you could have warned us, and you didn't because you thought we were too stupid to be told!' She was shaking with emotion. 'How dare you!'

The Doctor's face went ashen and he ran over to Amy, but he was brushed aside as Rory stepped between the two and wrapped his arms around Amy. He held her tightly, and she buried her head in his shoulder.

'He was called Albert,' Rory said quietly.

The Doctor paused, then nodded slowly. He reached out a hand to touch Amy's heaving shoulders but seemed to think better of it and withdrew. 'I'm sorry,' he said simply. 'I should have had more faith in you.'

'Yes, you should,' Rory agreed. 'Just give us a moment.'

The Doctor turned and walked slowly out into the hallway. Amy could see him leaning against the wall, rubbing his eyes with his sleeve. He looked tired, but then he screwed up his face in concentration. In the silence, Amy thought she could hear the noise of a plane in the distance.

A second later, the Doctor burst into the lounge once more. 'Wait, wait, wait!' he said.

Rory glared at him. 'I said give us a—'

'We haven't got time, Rory! What did you say the name of this town was?'

Rory shrugged. 'Appletown. But—'

'That's it! I knew it didn't make sense! What's the point of filling a town solely with robots that are designed to live amongst humans?' The Doctor slammed his fist against the wall. 'And the buildings! Flimsy wooden skeletons, barely convincing for any length of time. And no trees! It's a stopgap, something to keep the androids pacified, to stop them getting suspicious until...'

'Until what?' Amy asked.

The Doctor looked directly into her eyes, and Amy saw that he was scared, really, really scared. 'An Apple House is the term used by the US Army to describe the prefabricated buildings that were built for the testing of nuclear weapons during the 1960s.'

Realisation dawned on the pair.

'The clean-up operation,' Amy gasped.

'But it's *not* the 1960s,' Rory countered.

The Doctor held a finger to his lips and pointed at the ceiling with a long, thin finger. The group held their breath, and eventually the engine drone Amy had heard became more apparent. A heavy, hornet buzzing that was growing inexorably louder with every second.

'I think,' the Doctor said, 'that we should get back to the TARDIS.'

They were at the front door in an instant, Rory cannoning into it with such force that the wooden slab flew off its flimsy hinges and crashed onto the path outside. The Doctor tore ahead, then halted abruptly. Amy and Rory stepped out behind him, blinking around his silhouette as they tried desperately to see what he was looking at.

The front gate clanked softly in a light breeze and the bushes rustled gently, highlighting the terrifying silence that had fallen on the village. Amy's eyes scanned the street, falling across row upon row of impassive plastic faces. The villagers had gathered outside, waiting for them, but this time there wasn't a smile between them. She felt the Doctor's hand grasp hers and squeeze it tightly in an effort to stop her trembling.

'It's Isley,' she whispered in his ear. 'She found us.'

The young woman stood, head of the pack, on the other side of the garden gate. Her clunky headphones were snapped in two and each speaker hung limply across her chest from the connecting wire. Her hair was ruffled, but other than that she looked no different to when Amy had first encountered her in the attic. Amy felt her fear replaced with a cold anger as she realised the obvious ease with which the android must have dispatched Albert.

Isley cocked her head unnaturally and regarded the trio. 'You know,' she stated matter-of-factly.

The Doctor nodded slowly. 'Yes,' he said. 'We do.'

There was a pause.

'Run!' The Doctor yelled at the top of his voice.

Amy found herself pulled violently sideways towards the neatly trimmed privet hedge, and her hand slipped from the Doctor's as he vaulted into the next-door garden. Rory did the same and she scrambled to follow. She made the first jump with relative ease, again with the second and third, but on the fourth hedge she caught her boot in a branch and was sent sprawling flat on her face across the thin turf.

Rory heard her cry out and quickly turned to haul her to her feet. He tried not to look at the advancing crowd as she scrambled to her knees, instead snapping his head this way and that in search of the Doctor.

'Come on,' he told Amy gently as he heaved her upright. 'It's not that far.'

But when they turned again, the Doctor had vanished.

The Doctor had surprised himself with his own athleticism and felt a rush of adrenalin course through his body as hedges and fences swooped past beneath his boots in quick flashes of green and white. He whooped with triumph as he reached the end of the gardens and skidded into an alleyway that ran between the next block of houses and one of the large buildings he had seen when he first entered the village. Its rusty brown wooden cladding towered over him, casting a deep shadow over the houses at its feet and the Doctor could feel the sweat cool on his brow as he paused for breath. Confident that he had shaken his hunters for the time being, he turned to flash his companions an excited grin, but there was no one there.

'I've lost them *again*!' He ran a hand through his hair, and opened his mouth to shout. Then he thought better of attracting the attention of the pursuers he'd just lost. Then he felt guilty for not thinking of his companions first. Then he decided that if he was going to bring companions along on his travels he really should start taking better care of them. Finally he cupped his hands around his mouth and staggered in slow circles around the narrow alleyway as he shouted. 'Rory! Amy! Over here!'

There was no response. He opened his mouth to try again, but the words died in his throat as he circled once more and suddenly stopped short. There was a figure standing in the dark shadow of the building, an outline that was moving slowly towards him with an awkward, jerking motion. This wasn't the mechanical movement of an android; it was something much stranger, something unnatural, something completely wrong. Despite its stuttering motion there was still something familiar about that gait.

The Doctor opened his mouth in surprise as the figure made a final step towards him and a shaft of sunlight fell across its face from between the nearby houses, highlighting a gaunt, defined facial structure and a mop of foppish brown hair hanging limply across the man's forehead.

It was then that the Doctor realised that he was looking at himself.

Chapter

3

California International Conference Centre,
3 August 1975

Albert stumbled across the beach that bordered the Asilomar conference grounds, oblivious to the salt water that ebbed and flowed over his tatty leather shoes as he swerved in and out of the surf. He took another swig from the crystal bottle and wiped his face with his sleeve as the unbuttoned shirt cuff slapped at his face. Finding the bottle empty, he spun around in frustration, hurling it out to sea with a hoarse yelp and staggering on the spot for a second as he tried to spy the satisfying splash of it hitting the surface.

The light was fading and the glare of the

sunset, refracted a thousand times on the crests of the waves, dazzled him. He turned his back on the sea and loped back in the direction of the grassy dunes, spluttering an incomprehensible mix of anger and grief.

He ran out of balance at the steps to the wooden walkway, swearing as he slammed his shin against the first stair. He grabbed the handrail and swung himself awkwardly into a sitting position. The beach swam in front of him, but the tears in his eyes may have had something to do with that. He rested his head in his hands and listened to the steady roar of the sea as it lulled his pounding heart.

At least the sirens had stopped.

Behind him the flames had died down and the towering column of black smoke which had seemed so solid and impassive only an hour before was gradually dispersing.

Albert didn't bother trying to look up as the sound of footsteps clumping along the wooden planks of the walkway approached him. He fixed his eyes forward and concentrated on the nearest rock, making no acknowledgment of the presence behind him as the noise ceased.

'Dr Gilroy?' a gravelly voice enquired.

Albert mumbled something he hoped sounded in the affirmative.

'Dr Gilroy!' It wasn't a question, it was an order.

He turned his head and leant backward as he tried to take in the man who had so rudely interrupted his breakdown. Smart khaki trousers hung casually over polished black boots and there were no creases in the jacket that was belted tightly around the man's waist. Albert gave up trying to count the medals after he got to three and continued his attempt to force his eyes upwards to meet the man's stare, eventually finding himself glaring at a clipped moustache that seemed almost pasted onto a scarred and leathered face and eyes so grey that they matched his hair.

'What?' Albert finally managed to enunciate.

The man held out a large hand, and Albert allowed himself to be hauled to his feet. He stumbled backwards a few steps and jabbed his finger accusingly at the stranger. 'What?' he repeated.

The stranger waited patiently for a few moments as Albert felt for a spot on the handrail for support before continuing. 'Dr Gilroy, I am Colonel Geoffrey Redvers. You do not know me, but I am certainly aware of your work.'

Albert flung his arms up in exaggerated frustration. 'What work? Eh? What work? It's all gone now! If you want my work, you shouldn't be standing here; you should be sifting through the wreckage of the storeroom.' He gestured over to the tree line where smoke was still drifting between the branches. 'Burnt, all of it. Gone.' The enormity of the situation hit him once more and he wailed. 'And Isley! Did you know that I hadn't turned her off for over two years? Two years! And still so much to do.'

Geoff displayed no emotion. 'You can rebuild it,' he stated simply.

'Her.'

Geoff raised an eyebrow.

'Isley was a her.'

Geoff shrugged. 'You can rebuild *her*.'

Albert stepped forward and shoved him in the shoulder, looking for a fight. The man didn't budge. 'Oh yeah? And where am I gonna get funding from now, jackass? I'm a laughing stock. Completely discredited. No one in that conference centre believes that I ever had *anything*. And now they're right. I've nothing left but my notes, and they're not exactly a formal proof.'

'The notes you left in Michigan?' Geoff asked casually.

'Yes, the notes I left in Michigan.'

'Well, I'm afraid you don't have those either. My department picked them up this morning.'

Realisation dawned on Albert.

'Wait wait wait. *You* did this?' His hand flew to his face and he began to pace up and down the sand, the sun bathing him in a hazy golden glow. 'No. This isn't happening! You can't do this to me!'

Geoff sighed, 'I know that this has come as a bit of a blow. But I have a proposition for you.'

'I'm not stupid, Colonel. It's not a proposition. A proposition implies that I have a choice.'

'It's a lot of money.'

Albert's face hardened. 'It had better be.'

Geoff stepped off the bottom stair and onto the sand, walking around the bedraggled scientist. 'Come with me.' He tilted his head along the beach. 'There's a helicopter waiting in the bay. I presume you won't be wanting to say goodbye to your associates.'

Now that they were on a level it was obvious that the colonel towered a good foot over Albert. With his tight uniform highlighting his hefty build, he stood in stark contrast to the thin and unkempt figure beside him. Albert hunched his shoulders in defeat and reluctantly began to follow Geoff along the waterfront.

'No. My career is over. Disappearing is probably the most dignified thing to do.' He fumbled with the hem of his shirt as he tried in vain to tuck it back into his trousers. 'Yesterday I was going to be one of the most important men in history. Yesterday I was going to change the world. Today I am nothing.' He pointed back the way they had come. 'And no one even noticed. To them it's just another day of canapés and wine.'

'The world doesn't need changing just yet. A lot of people would rather it stayed just the way it is – at least until this country is ready.'

'And what makes you so sure that *you're* ready?'

Geoff shrugged. 'That's our job, to gain the advantage, to nip work like yours in the bud before our enemies notice that it even exists.'

'You mean the Russians.'

'Maybe. Everybody has the potential to be an enemy if you wait long enough. It's just a matter of time. And when that time comes, we'd like to be prepared.'

Albert didn't respond, and the pair walked in silence for a few minutes until they rounded the headland and the squat black shape of a helicopter came into view. A guard of four black-uniformed soldiers that had been standing casually around the makeshift landing strip suddenly acknowledged the approach of the colonel. They snapped to attention, saluting hurriedly as he strode past onto the landing strip.

The pilot started the rotors, and the helicopter

was barely stationary by the time Albert approached. The roar of the blades drowned out the urgent orders that were thrown around the site as the squad prepared to embark. One of the soldiers flung a helmet into his hand and he jammed it onto his head, ducking into the back of the cabin with Geoff. The pilot turned awkwardly in his seat and smiled at him. 'It's great to have you on board, sir.' He grinned.

Albert turned to look out of the window and offered no reply. 'I hope you know what you're doing,' he muttered over the radio.

'I was thinking the same thing about you,' came the crackled response.

A few seconds later, the chopper lifted off in a blizzard of sand and was soon pulling away from the headland and moving out to sea. As the craft swung around, Albert could still see smoke rising from the conference centre as the firemen extinguished the last of the flames, before the view slid softly away and he squinted his eyes against the dying embers of the sun.

Chapter
4

Colorado, 28 August 1981, 4.57 p.m.

Time paused, and the Doctor could feel it.

His whole body seemed to slow as he stepped towards the man he knew to be himself. Light flowed like a liquid in his vision as if the universe itself didn't want the two to meet, and the golden hue of the afternoon transformed into a haze that fogged his vision. The world became a dream, and in the centre stood two Doctors.

The Doctor screwed up his eyes and stumbled backwards, one, two steps, until the sensation eased and his mind began to focus again. He felt sick, but he was sure the other Doctor was waving at him.

'What do you want?' he managed to ask, squeezing his temples with his thumb and forefinger to try and clear the headache.

In response, the other Doctor held up an arm and pulled back his sleeve to reveal his gold watch. He twisted his wrist and turned the watch face towards the Doctor, pointing at it urgently. Then he opened his mouth.

'Teerrr ees ooon teeemm.'

The words were twisted and garbled, emphases in all the wrong places, a horrible, disturbing sound, and the Doctor could see the man was struggling to mouth the correct words.

A shiver ran down his spine as the other Doctor continued.

'Teer ees no teemm! Oorrri, Eeemi, tem leeiiv.'

'I don't understand! What are you trying to tell me, what's wrong?' The Doctor could sense the urgency in his double's voice. 'What's happened to me?'

'Teer eees no teemm!' the man repeated.

The Doctor suddenly understood. 'No time? Time for what?'

'Ooorrri, Eeemi, leeiivv tem.'

'Rory and Amy? Why? What's going to happen?' Now that his head had cleared, the Doctor could see the sweat glistening on the other Doctor's brow, the untidy chaos of his hair. Something had happened, something was going to happen. To him.

The other Doctor's sleeve seemed to pull itself back over the watch of its own accord as he extended his hand higher and pointed to the sky.

'Eeethe boomb.'

There was no mistaking that final word. The Doctor followed the man's finger and looked at the sky before letting out a yell of anguish. The dark shape of the plane was visible now as it circled overhead, a black vulture above the village, preparing for one final decent. The drone of its engines was louder now than it had ever been before.

'He's – I'm right, there's no time to go back before they drop the bomb.' He flexed his hands in frustration. 'But, I can't leave them! They'll die!'

The other Doctor shouted something that the Doctor couldn't comprehend, an unnatural warble of sound that ended with 'Taaaaarrdiz.'

'The TARDIS?'

'Cann zzdopp eet. Weel Zavay teeem.'

'What? How?' The Doctor's frustration was mounting. He was painfully aware of each relentless second that was ticking by whilst his double tried to communicate.

The other Doctor said nothing in response, instead feeling for his inside jacket pocket, the other hand smoothing his hair over his face. Eventually, the other Doctor found what he was looking for, flourishing open the psychic paper and holding it out for his opposite to view.

The Doctor stepped forward once more, wincing as the haze returned; he squinted through the suddenly heady glow of the sunlight, desperately trying to make out the faint diagrams that had imprinted themselves on the white slip. Eventually he stepped back, and his eyes met the other Doctor's.

'You're right,' he said finally. 'That could work. But the TARDIS has never done anything like that before. There's no telling the effect on the infrastructure – it could completely destabilise her!'

But the other Doctor seemed to have finished, holding up his hand to silence the Doctor. They looked at each other one last time, before the other Doctor shrugged his jacket off and into his hand before slinging it awkwardly over his shoulder.

'Wait, you can't go!' the Doctor called after him. 'What are you? My future? I would remember being you if you weren't, but if that's the case…' He swallowed uncomfortably and trailed off. 'What am I about to do?'

But the other Doctor had gone, shuffling backwards around a corner and looking about himself as if searching for someone else. Then the Doctor was alone in the alleyway once more. He rubbed his eyes as though waking from a deep sleep and walked forwards into the cool shade of the warehouse between the brutal shafts of light that glared from between the houses. Then the noise of the engines above invaded his mind and jolted him into action.

The Doctor's hefty boots pounded the sandy ground as the TARDIS came into view, the deep blue of its wooden frame an oasis amid the desert brown that surrounded it. He didn't slow as he covered the last few metres to the doors, key gripped in his hand, aimed at the lock.

Just in time, the double doors swung gently inwards, and the Doctor cannoned into the control room, his lungs shocked for a second by the sudden encounter with the TARDIS's air-conditioned environment.

He took the stairs by leaps and bounds, stumbling to the central console and splaying his hands across the panels as he reached for fourteen buttons and levers at once. The scanner snapped on in the wall behind him, a detailed three-dimensional model of the surroundings, searching and scanning for the plane above the town. It found it, and the model immediately split into a shower of possible trajectories and velocities, one strand highlighted in red, as the digital image of an atom bomb began to descend.

But the TARDIS was already in flight. The Doctor whirled around the console, seemingly propelling himself from lever to lever simply with the force of each movement. 'Come on, come on, right spot, right time, we can do it you sexy, sexy thing!'

He brought a fist down on a control panel hard, and the howl of the engines exploded into a scream. Yanking the smaller view-screen around with him, the Doctor suddenly swapped sides and paused, eyes transfixed on the readouts that swam across his vision faster than anyone human could have comprehended. His fingers tapped feverishly on the side of the monitor as he muttered under his breath. 'Seven, six, five, four, three, two, one...' Pause. 'Now!' The last word was punctuated by a brutal kick to the underside of the console.

It clanged loudly, the reverberations echoing around the towering control room for seconds after the impact, and when the Doctor had stopped nursing his injured foot he realised that the engines had ceased.

Gingerly he rested his foot back onto the glass floor and, painfully slowly, lifted his eyes to the ceiling.

Hanging barely a foot from the Doctor's head was the bomb. A large, ugly heap of metal engulfed in a static ball of energy, white hot fire frozen abruptly at its highest velocity, halted only a few centimetres from his upturned face. Behind the bubble, its reflection in the metal ripples that arced away from the central column cast a thousand tiny suns around the control room.

He stared in wonderment at the object for a moment, then a slow grin spread across his face. 'I did it,' he said to himself. 'I only went and did it!'

Hesitantly, he raised his hand up to the object, transfixed by its violent beauty.

Suddenly, the calm hue of the control room switched to a dark crimson as an urgent alarm blared loudly out of the gramophone speaker on the console. He snatched his hand away. 'All right, all right, I get the point.' He scowled, reaching out to press a key. 'It's not often one gets to see an atomic explosion at the point of detonation.' But his sulk was swiftly replaced by a worried frown as the siren continued. He looked back at the ball of energy, opening his mouth in horror as, agonisingly slowly, the flames of light began to swirl within the confines of the force bubble.

Time hiccupped, and the bubble's diameter expanded by a millimetre as the TARDIS groaned under the strain of containment. The Doctor found himself thrown against the railings of the console by an incredible shockwave.

'Stasis leak.' He struggled to breathe as his arms flailed across the hard metal floor that strobed beneath him in the red light. 'I have to get out of here.'

His body twisted and convulsed as the atmosphere began to boil, suffocating him as he pawed his way along the floor towards the doors. His arms trembled and shook with the effort required to pull his body even an inch, and by the time his fingers were scrabbling at the edge of the wooden panelling his face was drenched with sweat. Tears of exertion ran down his cheeks as he prised open the latch and the door inched slowly open. It took his last ounce of strength to fling his body over the threshold and onto the stony desert ground beyond.

'We've lost the Doctor!' Amy shouted as she tried to catch her breath. 'What is he doing?'

'It doesn't matter. We know the route; we can meet him at the TARDIS.' Rory looked over his shoulder. 'That is, if we manage to keep all our limbs until we get there.'

The citizens of Appletown were swarming along the street towards them, spilling over into the gardens Rory and Amy had passed through only seconds before. No longer attempting to appear human, the androids clambered over fences and through hedges with an almost insect-like movement of limbs that contrasted grotesquely with their pastel fashion sense. Amy nearly retched as she watched one woman, sporting a fetching mini dress that she would have killed for, get caught awkwardly in one of the fences as it collapsed beneath her, only to free herself through a 360-degree rotation of her forearms that twisted the rubber skin around her elbows until it ripped to expose the steel skeleton beneath.

She turned and headed straight for the garden gate, leaping into the road to dodge a pair of grasping hands and rolling back onto her feet, nearly losing her balance as she pushed forward to try and outrun her pursuers. She could hear Rory panting behind her as they rounded the street corner and the large Appletown sign loomed up in front of them.

She picked up the pace for one last sprint to the TARDIS as Rory drew alongside, the final few houses hurtling past as they pelted down the street. Three, two, one, the last buildings fell away and they entered the open desert, sand and rocks stretching for miles in every direction, the horizon a haze that blurred into the pale blue sky, and that was all there was.

'But…' Amy panted as her lungs burned and she slowed in bewilderment.

'It was there. It was right there!' Rory said.

But it wasn't any longer, and Amy rushed to the shallow dent in the ground that was the only indication the TARDIS had ever been there at all. She stood in the centre of the square and flung her arms up in frustration.

'Doctor!' she shouted. 'Come back!'

They stood in silence for a moment, their ears straining for the familiar sound of the engines, but there was nothing but the wind and the faint drone of the plane as it passed over the village.

Rory scanned the sky for the aircraft in puzzlement. 'I thought the Doctor was implying that we were about to be nuked,' he said. 'But the plane is leaving and we're still alive.'

'Well, thank heavens for small mercies,' Amy snapped. 'In the meantime we're stuck in the desert with nothing for miles but a town full of homicidal robots for company.'

Rory looked over his shoulder nervously, expecting a hoard of villagers to emerge from the buildings any second.

'I think we should get as far away from here as possible,' he suggested, but Amy shook her head solemnly.

'The Doctor wouldn't leave us behind. He'll

come back – and when he does we need to be here.'

Rory shuffled uncomfortably. 'But there's got to be some sort of human outpost somewhere, some sort of observation tower for the testing.'

'I'm sure there is, but it'll be miles out of range of an atomic blast and we have no idea what direction it's in,' Amy retorted. 'We could just be walking deeper into the desert, how long do you think we'll be able to survive out in the open in this heat? And that's not even considering the fact that we'd be sitting ducks to Isley and her friends out in the open.'

'OK, OK, you've made your point.'

Amy sniffed, and silence descended once more.

'I guess we should try and find somewhere to hide then.' Rory suggested eventually. 'If we stay out of their way long enough, maybe the citizens will reset.'

'Considering what's happened so far, I wouldn't bet on it being so easy,' Amy said as she strode past him. 'Come on,' she said, 'we'll circle around and enter from the east.'

Rory looked around. 'Which way is east?'

'I don't know, it just sounded better than "a different direction to the one we came in by", that's all.'

Rory undid another button on his shirt and reluctantly began to follow her, glancing over his shoulder with every step. He couldn't shake the feeling that they were being watched.

Chapter
5

Utah Military Research Base, 27 May 1977

'Coffee?'

'What? Oh yeah, sure. Put it by the limbs.'

Albert didn't bother to look up as Geoff entered the workshop that the majority of the base had nicknamed 'the magician's palace'. It certainly looked the part, with great swathes of coloured polythene, clothes and sheets of plastic flesh hung from wires all around the central workspace. The tamer items stood near the doorway: wooden crates filled with robotic limbs, polished arms and hands complete with bolted aluminium fingers hanging limply over the edge of the boxes, independent generators whirring gently and making the hands twitch in a scarily lifelike manner every few minutes.

Further inside were rows of shelves containing a large number of human-like heads – metal skulls coated in the cutting edge of plastic technology. Rubber eyelids lay carefully over gel eyeballs and the only hint of the microchip technology that stood in for a brain was the open hatch above the right ear on every model and the soft blue glow pulsating from within.

The back wall displayed the various readouts, charts and graphs that were being fed out from the small, handheld device in Albert's palm. Only fifteen centimetres square, the box contained the entire processing power and coding that had, four years ago now, once taken up the entire computer lab at Michigan University, and which in turn was connected by a spray of wires to the centrepiece of the whole operation:

The android.

The flickering readouts rippled across the metal skeleton, catching its steel bolts and reflecting tiny points of light around the room. This one was a woman, a baggy T-shirt slung over the unskinned torso protected her inner workings, but her head was almost human. Her round face sported a wide pair of big blue eyes, a freckly nose and ruby lips all framed by a short, sandy bob to complete the illusion. Isley II.

If Albert had any emotional attachment to the robot he didn't show it, instead wiggling specific wires with the end of his biro and flicking his eyes to the screen in search of a change in the data, repeating the process at least twice for each connection.

Geoff was used to being ignored by the scientist, especially now that the delivery dates, which had seemed so far away only a month ago, were looming perilously close.

'And the admin girls and boys upstairs want you to turn your music down. They can hear it over three floors.'

Albert gave up switching the wires and dropped the device on a nearby table, scratching his ear with the pen. 'Really? Would they prefer to listen to me swearing and drilling? I'd take Cher over that any day.'

'Well, maybe just mix up the cassettes occasionally.'

The scientist sucked through his teeth as he took a swig from the polythene cup. 'Sheesh, people have no taste any more.' He looked down at his coffee. 'Speaking of which, what roast is this?'

'We're out; I had to use the canteen stuff.'

Albert ran his tongue over his mouth in disgust. 'Warn me next time,' he said.

Geoff moved forward into the lab and began to inspect the android carefully. He waved a hand in front of its face, but the eyes didn't follow it. He raised the other hand – nothing again. Suddenly he clapped both hands together, and the rubber eyelids blinked involuntarily. Albert carefully perched his drink on the workbench with his control box and walked over to join him.

'Only her involuntary reflexes are switched on at the moment. I'm still trying to refine the trigger from standard to military mode and I don't want her trying to kill me if I get it wrong,' he said.

Geoff nodded and reached out to touch Isley's face, but the scientist slapped it away.

'No touching!'

Geoff did as he was told. 'To be honest, I didn't expect you to go so quietly when we asked you to implement the military programming,' he said gruffly.

Albert sighed. 'I wasn't exactly surprised, considering who's bankrolling me. I presumed robot-soldiers would be on the agenda from the start. At least this way I can also work on the civilian AI model simultaneously. *That's* the magical part. With the technology you boys had already, it wouldn't have been hard to create an android that just kills people. But I can make an android so lifelike that it can appear to be human for days, even weeks before it's triggered to kill – that's the key. And making a human-like machine is what I've always dreamt of. So I guess I'm happy.' He shrugged.

Geoff looked at him earnestly. 'It's not all bad. Think of the lives we can save when we don't have to put human beings in danger. If we can create an assassin, of any nationality, with full combat training – a smooth and effective kill, no collateral damage and no US citizen put at risk.'

Albert matched his gaze. 'Yeah and think of all the other people we might decide suddenly need assassinating once it becomes a risk-free venture.'

Geoff turned away. 'Our job is to keep people safe, Albert, not to terrorise the world.'

'Keep telling yourself that.' Albert picked up the control box once more and swapped a couple of wires around before screwing the back plate on tighter.

Taking that as a sign that the conversation was over, Geoff walked towards the exit, but paused with his hand on the door handle. He turned back.

'Hey, uh, have you seen *Star Wars* yet?' he asked. 'I know it's only been out a week…'

Albert raised his eyebrows. 'No, I've not left the building in three days.'

Geoff looked suddenly sheepish. 'It's just, I've

got a couple of spare tickets, thought you might want to come along.'

'Why'd you get spare tickets?'

'They weren't spare when I got them. I bought one for Marge and one for Sally.'

'Oh… And why aren't they going?'

Geoff's military façade shattered for a moment as he choked up and suddenly Albert no longer saw his boss. In his place was a man who looked a shadow of his former self: drawn and grey and very, very tired.

'She left me this morning,' was all the soldier could manage before he turned and walked quickly out of the laboratory.

Chapter

6

Colorado, 28 August 1981, 5.15 p.m.

The smell of smoke made the Doctor cough as he gradually regained consciousness. Blearily, he opened his eyes and realised his clothes were smouldering. Pale white trails were rising from beneath his body and, as he raised an arm to shield his face from the sun, he noticed that his sleeves had blackened along the back. 'Oh, swear,' he said half-heartedly, dropping his head back to the ground and waiting for his strength to return.

He gazed into the deep blue of the afternoon sky and wondered how long he'd been unconscious, and whether it was long enough to get a tan.

Then his memory came crashing back.

The Doctor sat bolt upright. He reached a hand up to his face and winced as he realised it was sunburnt. That long? This wasn't good.

Getting to his feet, he looked around quickly. The TARDIS stood, an incongruous monolith, in the exact centre of Appletown. Roads radiated out from the town's central space like the spokes of a giant wheel. He looked to the sky in admiration; the bomber pilot must have been extremely skilled to perform so accurate a delivery.

He walked over to the TARDIS, slipping off his jacket and wrapping it around his fist as he reached out to touch the sturdy wood of the frame.

He was surprised when he found it quite cool to the touch and quickly unwrapped his hand before placing his palm flat against one of the panels. 'That's strange,' he said. 'You must be dissipating the energy.' He paused for a second and frowned. 'I wonder how.'

He scanned his surroundings once more, but this part of the town was eerily quiet and he quickly realised that he hadn't managed to explore this far before. He took a moment to get his bearings before deciding on which direction he would find his waiting companions. He needed to get them back to the TARDIS as soon as possible – there was was no telling how long the stasis field would hold.

He spun on his heel and walked in the opposite direction to the one that he had intended.

Within five minutes the Doctor was lost. He looked at his watch, then up at the third identical row of houses he had passed in as many minutes, then back at his watch, then up again. Something wasn't right, but he wasn't sure which it was, the watch or the houses?

He looked at the timepiece on his wrist more closely, peering at the three hands as they rotated slowly across the gold roman numerals, the second hand smoothly counting down; six, five, four, three, two, one, twelve…

It was running backwards.

The Doctor considered the implications. He scanned the rooftops of Appletown, holding his wrist against his ear as he listened for any noise that might indicate a loose cog in the mechanism of his timepiece. Then he recognised a familiar shape through the white haze: the dark outline of the warehouse he had stood under only a few minutes before, the warehouse where he had met himself.

He dawdled in the road for a second, eyeing up the building with uncharacteristic hesitancy. Abruptly he held up a finger, as if preparing to make an excuse as to why he really, really shouldn't go and test his troubling theory, but found he had nothing to say. He scratched at his forearm where his rolled-up shirt sleeves had left the rough material of his jacket to itch his skin, and then made up his mind. He shoved the hand with the watch into his pocket and walked on.

A few moments later he was skirting the sunny side of the building, looking this way and that in search of what he hoped he wouldn't find. He passed the large, bolted wooden doors of the warehouse and felt a chill run down his spine that was more than just the sun being blotted from view. Then he saw him, his past self, standing open-mouthed and gazing right at the spot that the Doctor had appeared from.

'OK, OK, bear with me,' he muttered as he slipped his jacket over his shoulder and shrugged it on, but his past self didn't seem to understand and stepped forward. 'Nope, you wait right there. I remember that headache.' He held up a hand and shuffled his pockets for the psychic paper. 'And I remember how this went, so let's just get on with it.'

His fingers felt the soft leather wallet and he pulled it out, trying to picture the maze of buttons and levers that had performed the stasis miracle on the bomb as it imprinted itself onto the slip. He started as his past self warbled something incomprehensible and anguished, a blur of sound.

'Koow duk tat. Tiiir rowu,' he finished.

'Yeah, whatever you say.' The Doctor flipped open the wallet and held it out for his other self to see, but his face fell when he saw his past self's blank expression.

'Right, backwards communication, how do you do this?' His mind raced to try and map his sentences onto a soundscape that would make sense in reverse. He swallowed and opened his mouth. 'You can save them, you can save them, stop it,' he whispered, practicing quickly to himself before beginning.

'Meeth Yarvas, te dops nack.' He raised his eyebrows to see if he had managed to convey anything that made any sense, before realising that the reaction to his sentence would have preceded his speech anyway.

'ZZidart heathe?' his past self responded.

The Doctor knew what that meant.

'The zzzidart, yes, use the TARDIS, the instructions I've given you, I mean, am about to give you, they're for the TARDIS!' He spoke slowly and loudly like a tourist in a foreign country with no grasp of the native language. 'You've got to use them now! You can save them from the nuke! I mean... bmobe heathe!' He shouted over the other

Doctor's tirade of nonsense, pointing to the sky with urgency.

'Oh my days, I really didn't make an effort back then, did I?' he muttered to himself.

Luckily the next words his past self spoke were more comprehensible. 'Iirore, Yima.'

The Doctor raised his eyes to the sky. 'Thank heavens for companions with nearly palindromic-sounding names!' he said.

'Leave them, meathe veal, Iirore, Yima. Meet on see reathe!' Sadness crept over him then as he remembered hearing the words he was speaking now, and the false hope that they had implanted in his mind. 'You know what, past me?' he said quietly. 'The terrible thing is, despite what I'm saying, I don't know if they live or die. I have no idea what terrible things might happen to them in our future. But there's one thing I do know, and it's that we'll *all* die if you don't *get a move on*!' He yanked his sleeve down and pointed to his watch. 'Meet! Own! See! Reathe!' he yelled. 'Now go!'

But his past self just stood there, recognition fading from his face. The Doctor looked at him and realised that his words had already conveyed their importance long before he'd even arrived.

'Sorry,' he said. 'There's no point shouting at you now, you've done what I asked already and right now you have my entire life to live backwards through. But I'm not sticking around to watch that all over again, I'm going. I'm going, and I'll fix this.' He paused. 'I promise, Doctor, I'll fix this.' With a curt wave, he stumbled backwards along the alleyway, away from his past self, into the shadows and out of the other Doctor's sight. He watched mournfully as he saw his past self stumble backwards and begin to circle, shouting his companions' names backwards at the top of his voice. Then he turned and walked away.

'It was a good idea, a very good idea.' The Doctor strode back into the central square, and began to pace up and down in front of the TARDIS. 'Go back on our time line and dissipate the energy gradually rather than letting it all be released instantaneously in the future. Safer for you, yes, and for me, if it works.' He pointed an accusing finger at the inanimate time machine. 'But how long does it take to diffuse an atomic explosion? Tell me that? It had better be soon enough, because look at this.' He cupped his hand and turned it upside down, flicking his gaze from the ground to the TARDIS as a small cloud of sand lifted itself from the dusty road and ascended towards his palm, spilling into his hand as he turned it, unpouring the dust that he would soon scoop from the desert floor.

Then time froze, and stuttered.

For an instant the sand hung in mid air, tiny grains sparkling as they caught the sun and the Doctor crouched to inspect the shimmering trail that linked his palm and the road. 'See?' He whispered, and broke the spell. The sand flashed quickly through various states of suspension, then hissed onto the floor once more. 'The universe does not appreciate a man whose effects precede his cause.' He straightened up. 'And it's not going to put up with it for ever.'

The Doctor patted the side of the TARDIS and turned to leave. 'You just do the best you can,' he said.

He turned his face to the sky, searching for the bomber as it glided backwards, retracing its approach over Appletown. The plane would've passed over the military observation tower en route to the target for a last-minute visual on the situation. He could follow the flight path.

If the bomb wasn't going to detonate, then he'd need to warn the troops.

Chapter

7

Florida Airbase, 3 February 1980

The grey expanse of tarmac stretched as far as the eye could see and shimmered in the pale glow of a low-slung winter sun. Albert emerged, blinking, from the shadowy confines of the hangar, scratching his eyes as they readjusted to a three-dimensional reality after his twelve-hour shift at the monitors.

He stuffed his hands in his lab coat and strode away from the steel building. Through the haze of the horizon he could already see the black dot of the helicopter as it approached. Behind him he could hear the sound of jeeps hissing on the dewy tarmac as they approached, but he kept his gaze fixed on the aircraft.

Car doors slammed behind him. A squad of soldiers taking point around the designated landing area and suddenly Geoff was at his side.

'Any idea what happened?' he said, wiping the condensation from his moustache.

'Her pass wasn't cleared at the embassy and she thought her cover was blown. I don't know the exact details; it's chaos on the monitors. She just went rogue.'

'This isn't good,' said Geoff.

'No, it isn't.'

The noise of the rotors drowned out the rest of their conversation, and Geoff's hat was sent skittering away across the airfield. Albert wrapped his lab coat tighter around him in the sudden chill, the hems billowing in the breeze. His wispy hair pulled away from his face as he stepped forward to greet the sergeant who was ducking out from the helicopter hatch. They shook hands briefly.

'Is she in there?' Albert nodded towards the rear of the aircraft.

'Yes sir. I'm hesitant to move her out of the Electro-Magnetic Field though, she's pretty badly beaten up and the civilian-reset won't work if her innards are on display. I'm not gonna mess you about, it was a nightmare getting her off-site.'

'You did good, Sergeant,' Geoff interjected.

The sergeant saluted. 'Just doing my job, sir.'

'We can take it from here,' Albert said. 'This'll sort out the reset issue.' He pulled a chunky box from his coat pocket, attached to which were a pair of headphones. The sergeant looked puzzled. 'It's a Walkman,' Albert explained. 'They're all the rage. Where've you been? Now, if you'll just release her. Please,' he added.

The sergeant turned and gestured to the pilot to shut off the spinning blades before approaching the helicopter once more. He opened the rear hatch and turned to look over his shoulder at the two men. 'The EM field extends nearly to your feet, so be ready with the headphones.'

Albert nodded.

A figure stepped out of the hatch: a young female with a sandy bob and freckled nose.

Geoff turned to Albert and raised an eyebrow. 'You didn't tell me you sent Isley in,' he murmured.

Albert ignored him.

The sergeant offered the woman a hand as she stepped down to the concrete, but she brushed it away, stumbling as her feet touched the ground and her legs struggled to bear her weight. It was plain to see why. He legs were in tatters, swathes of plastic hanging limply from the dented exoskeleton beneath, and her shorts were filled with bullet holes. The sergeant had draped his regulation jacket over her shoulders and Albert was relieved at that. He had no wish to see the damage underneath.

Isley looked around uncertainly for a second. Only one gel-pupil had adjusted to the light; the other was clouded over. She spotted the men and gave an awkward smile of recognition. Wresting her twitching hand from the hatch-frame she started towards the pair, her left leg wobbling strangely with every step.

The soldiers on point tracked the limping figure slowly and silently as she crossed the tarmac towards her creator. Nobody made a sound, nobody breathed.

Albert smiled encouragingly. 'Welcome home, darling,' he said.

Her legs gave out two metres before she could reach the pair, and she dropped to her hands and knees with a crunch of metal.

Albert ran forward to help her, holding the back of her head with his hand and tilting it so that he could look into her face.

'She's outside the EM field, Albert, be careful,' Geoff called out.

'She won't switch to military mode if you don't mention that she's a robot,' Albert called back.

There was an abrupt rattle as every soldier

cocked his weapon. The deadly word had been uttered.

'It's all right, it's all right! I've got it.' Gently, Albert slipped the headphones over the woman's ears before she could trigger and clicked the play button on the Walkman. 'I was just testing you.' He winked at the stony faces around him.

Geoff's body blocked the light as he peered over Albert's shoulder. 'What's that then?'

'The Isley Brothers. Puts her in a neutral state so I can interface with the military and civilian programs without her trying to kill me.'

'Any particular reason it has to be the Isley Brothers?'

Albert sighed. 'Because I like them and I'd rather listen to them than modulated static whilst I'm working. Get some imagination, Geoff.' He pushed a finger behind the woman's ear and her maintenance hatch popped open. From his other pocket he produced a tiny microphone and slipped the plug into a socket on her skull before tapping her head sharply as if testing a sound system. 'Isley? Isley, sweetheart, can you hear me?'

Isley's mouth moved silently for a second before her voice box synced up. 'Yes, Albert, I can.'

'Good stuff, well done, girl. Now me and the colonel need to ask you a few questions. Is that OK?'

'Yes, of course,' she responded.

'Good.' Albert handed the microphone to his partner, feeding the wire over his shoulder.

'Isley,' said Geoff. 'Tell me what happened in Cuba. Our information is scrambled.'

Isley turned her head to look at Geoff with a puzzled frown on her face. 'I did as requested. I located the target, but my cover was compromised and I switched to military mode as per my programming.'

'Yes, yes, we know all that. But did you kill the target?'

'The target was one of the people I executed.'

Albert and Geoff swapped an uneasy glance.

'*One* of the people?' Geoff asked.

'I executed all witnesses that were aware of my... nature.'

Albert snatched the microphone back, Isley's impassive face turning to follow it.

'Wait, wait,' he said. 'Those weren't your orders. We were standing by to airlift you out once you destroyed the target – it didn't matter if your cover was blown after that. Why didn't you just destroy the target?'

'I was not aware that only the target was specifically designated for execution. I was programmed to locate the target and switch to military mode, that is all.'

'What?' Geoff was shocked. 'Albert, why didn't you *specifically* program her to kill the target?'

'Because we didn't know what the target *looked* like at that time! I had no information to give her that would isolate him amongst the other victims.'

Geoff stepped backwards and began pacing back and forth in front of the android. 'Oh, this is brilliant, just brilliant. Our heads are going to be on the block for this, you know that? We're going to be burned at the stake.'

Albert ignored him and leaned in towards Isley, speaking hurriedly. 'Isley, you need to tell me how many people you executed. It's very important.' He looked at Geoff. 'Look, if it's one or two, we'll be fine; it's not a big deal.'

'It's still one or two more people than we should've killed!' Geoff snapped. He put his hand to his forehead. 'Dear Lord, think of the paperwork,' he muttered.

'Fifty.'

The pair swung their heads to look at the android.

'Wait, what was that?' Albert's voice trembled into the microphone.

'Fifty. I terminated fifty witnesses,' Isley repeated impassively.

The microphone shattered as it was thrown to

the tarmac with the full force of Albert's strength. He swore, he swore long and hard and loud, and he didn't stop swearing for a good two hours after that.

Chapter
8

Colorado, 28 August 1981, 5.38 p.m.

Amy didn't breathe and, apart from the occasional grunt as he shuffled across the lawn beneath the garden hedge, neither did Rory. Their initial hopes that the androids might have forgotten about them had been dashed almost immediately as they attempted to re-enter Appletown, discovering almost too late that the residents had fanned out with military precision and were sweeping across the village with relentless ease. Rory had grabbed her and pulled her to the ground in someone's back garden as he saw Isley's sinister outline staring out from an upstairs window, and they had proceeded to shuffle flat on their stomachs through the terraced hedges and lawns from then on.

'These stains will never, ever come out,' Rory hissed as he looked mournfully down at his pale blue shirt, which was now streaked a dirty green and brown.

'Is that all you can think of right now? I'll buy you a new one if we get out of this alive, how about that?'

'Sounds fair,' Rory muttered.

They reached the corner of the next hedge, and Amy curled up as small as possible in the nook, out of sight of anyone passing by on the road that lay on the other side of the greenery. She encouraged Rory to do the same. They'd run out of back garden.

'We're going to have to cross the road.' Rory's face fell.

'Give us a second,' Amy whispered back. 'I need to catch my breath.'

Rory reached out and touched her shoulder comfortingly. 'Take your time,' he said.

Amy tilted her head back and edged it up in an attempt to see over the top of the hedge, before yanking it back down again, just in case. 'What I don't understand,' she said, 'is how we outran them before – they're machines for God's sake, we should have been murdered the moment we stopped to look for the TARDIS. And then it's like, the moment we started to move back inside the village, they were swarming all over the place again.'

Rory rubbed his chin. 'Yeah, I was thinking about that,' he answered. 'And you know what? I think they wanted us to escape.' Amy gave him a withering glare. He held up a placating hand. 'Bear with me. Look, they were reset when we got here, right? Well, now they're awake they probably have even less of an idea where we are than *we* do. I think they were testing us, trying to see if we would lead them to civilisation – it must be a nightmare for a bunch of robot spies to be without the full information.'

Amy rested her head against the hedge behind her and sighed as its leaves bowed comfortably around her. 'So I guess now that we've proved we have absolutely nothing to offer them, they won't be so lenient next time.'

'Well, it's just a theory.' Rory shrugged.

Amy was silent for a second, gathering her thoughts. 'OK, enough. We're freaking ourselves out here. Let's just get somewhere safe until the Doctor arrives. I don't want to think about anything else right now.'

It was Rory's turn to peer over the hedge now. The faint smell of leaves and general atmosphere of freshly cut grass seemed oddly comforting considering the circumstances. He'd never encountered danger in an environment that reminded him so much of home before, and it was a chilling thought to consider that such things could happen on any street – even his.

'Let's go,' he muttered, and they did, dashing over to the gate, fingers holding the catch so as not to make a noise then ducking out across the junction towards the opposite block of houses. Rory snapped his head back the way they had come as Amy struggled with the catch on the next gate. He looked around: more houses, the warehouse, garden after identical front garden and, standing motionless in the middle of the road, Isley – two blocks away and looking straight at him. He did a double take, not quite certain whether he was seeing things, and in that moment she flashed him a smile.

'Gotcha,' she mouthed and suddenly she was in motion, sprinting at full pelt towards them, no acceleration, no build-up, zero to twenty miles per hour in the time it took for Rory to blink.

He threw himself after Amy, a sliding tackle into the gate as she moved to hide behind the hedge, grabbing her sleeve as his legs scraped across the ground, grit scratching at his calves.

'She's found us. Get inside the house!' Rory

yelled. Amy dithered. 'Now!'

He ran to the nearest bay window, turning his head away and flinching even before his elbow hit the polished pane. There was a thud and tinkle of glass that sounded far too gentle for the pain Rory experienced as the impact shot up his arm. Then he was bundling Amy in through the splintered window frame as fast as he could.

'What about the front door?' Amy squealed as she tumbled onto a bare wooden floor.

'If it was locked, we'd have been dead before I broke it down,' Rory responded as his hefty body was cushioned by hers.

She heaved him off her and jumped to look out of the window as a ripple of noise spread across the village. Front doors slammed across Appletown, a silent alarm had been raised and the villagers were descending on their prey.

Rory scanned the room for anything useful but, like the Sandersons' house, the lounge was furnished only with an awful beige sofa and a modest television set.

'What if someone had been in here?' Amy shouted. 'We could've been walking into a trap!'

Rory threw up his hands in exasperation. 'Now is not the time to be talking, dear! Just get out of the back door now!'

They ran across the hallway towards the rear

of the house, through the open-plan kitchen and towards the large glass double doors that led out into the back garden.

One of the doors was ajar.

The pair halted at the sound of a voice.

'You didn't tell me we had guests dear.'

'I didn't?' another voice replied from the garden. 'Well, that must have been because I wasn't expecting any.'

A woman stepped into view on the other side of the glass panelling, the paisley-patterned picture of a perfect housewife who was joined on her right by a moustachioed, dungaree-wearing gardener, complete with tanned skin, sleek black hair and a chest that looked like it could house wildlife.

'Back!' Rory yelled.

But the front door was also blocked. Isley's dark shape blotted out the light that should have streamed through the frosted windows, and a loud hammering began as her fists beat out a deadly rhythm on the wood panelling outside.

Rory looked at Amy smugly. 'See, it *was* locked.'

But Amy was already pounding up the stairs to the floor above. She turned at the top of the landing to see Rory still dawdling in the hallway.

'What are you doing?' she yelled.

Rory looked up at her then dashed through the

open door to the lounge. There was a crash that made Amy flinch; the sound of glass cascading to the kitchen floor as the sinister couple switched off their house-proud personas. In the confusion, she barely registered that the drumbeat on the front door had ceased.

Rory returned a moment later, struggling up the stairs towards the frightened girl and swaying under the weight of the bulky television set. He chipped its wood cladding on the banister as he clambered upwards. 'Find a bedroom with lots of furniture, we'll barricade ourselves in!' His voice was muffled by the large object.

'What's that for? Passing the time while they try to break in?' Amy was scared and confused.

'Just get in a room and get ready. I'm going to buy us some time.' He reached the last stair and turned just in time to see the housewife and her husband standing impassively at the foot of the staircase, heads tilted in unison, regarding the young man with a piercing gaze.

'There really is no point to all this fussing, young man.' The woman placed a brown-slippered foot onto the first wooden step. 'You're only wasting your own time.' She rested a hand on the banister and began to climb the stairs as if embarking on the most mundane of upstairs tidying.

Rory hefted the television over his head,

stepping backwards in an attempt to keep his balance. He locked his arms and heaved the set in a wide arc that sent the heavy wooden box crashing down onto the surprised head of the android. The vacuum tube imploded, and Rory made a vain attempt to shield his face with his sleeve from the shards of glass and wood that streamed outwards from the figure as she was sent sprawling back towards her husband by the force of the blast. Some smaller splinters skipped through his fingers and Rory screwed up his face as a sharp cut slashed across his cheek, missing his eye by millimetres.

At the foot of the staircase, the woman clenched her fist and, unflinchingly, began beating at the wooden frame that still covered her face, splintering it after only a few blows. The metal rivets and panelling tumbled to the floor in a pile of sawdust and scrap metal.

The woman turned her head once more to face the shocked pair who stood open-mouthed only a few metres above her. Amy gasped.

Where once had been the friendly face of a housewife, with permed hair and laughter lines, there was now nothing but a metal skull. The glass of the television screen had shredded the rubber skin completely, and sparking wires sprayed out from between the steel bones. One of her gel-eyeballs was still in its socket, and it swivelled slowly to meet Amy's horrified gaze.

Casually, the husband tossed the remains of the set back into the lounge and shoved his wife to one side as what was left of the woman's hand felt roughly about for the banister. But Amy was already being bundled into a nearby bedroom, Rory slamming the door shut behind them and leaping to grab the top of a nearby wardrobe as he did so. His feet lifted from the floor as he attempted to use the weight of his body to tip it over across the frame.

Amy spotted a desk in the far corner and began dragging it across, just as the wardrobe crashed into place. Rory moved over to help her heave it onto the top.

'This isn't going to hold them five minutes,' Amy panted.

'Well, I'm out of other ideas,' Rory responded. 'They don't seem to appreciate having their disguises destroyed though; maybe they'll take the time to devise an approach which doesn't involve them losing half their skin.'

He was interrupted by the steady clump of feet from the other side of the barricaded door as the husband's heavy gardening boots made their way across the landing.

'Then again...' Rory held up his hands. 'I'm

probably wrong.'

There was the squeak of a door handle being turned and the pair froze, eyes fixed on the silver bar of metal. But it remained stationary.

'Next door.' Amy breathed.

She was right. There was a soft thud as the bedroom door to their left was closed again gently, then the footsteps resumed until they shuffled to a halt right in front of the terrified couple.

Another squeak, and this time the handle moved. It angled downwards slowly and there was a solid thump as the door encountered the wardrobe a second later. It rattled in frustration for a second, then the handle slipped slowly back into its original position.

Rory sighed as the footsteps began to retreat down the stairs once more. 'Then again...' He mimicked his previous gesture. 'I could be right after all.'

'Why do I always panic a little bit whenever you say things like that?' Amy's tone was chiding, but she wriggled under her fiancé's arm and held him tightly.

'I hope you're not talking about those frozen pies we had in September,' Rory replied half-heartedly. 'Because if you are, it's your fault for throwing the packaging out before I had a chance to read the cooking instructions.' He paused. 'And you were only sick for a day – I had to take the week off work.'

Amy grunted in reply as her attention was diverted by Rory's arm, hung lazily over her shoulder. She grabbed it with both hands and examined it animatedly. 'Babes, you're bleeding!' she cried.

Rory looked down. 'Oh yeah,' he said, inspecting his arm as if seeing it for the first time. The striped sleeve of his shirt had been shredded by fragments of the television and beneath the tattered fabric his forearm was criss-crossed with gently weeping red scratches. 'I didn't notice that before.' He screwed up his face. 'It hurts like hell!' He winced as he gently drew the cuff away from his arm and licked his thumb in a half-hearted attempted to clean himself up.

Amy batted his faltering fingers away and took over. 'We haven't got time for you to play the squeamish nurse, Rory. Grit your teeth and imagine you're bandaging up any other patient – and do it quickly!'

Rory raised an open palm and made a face as if she were stupid. 'And what exactly am I supposed to tie it up with?'

In response, Amy grabbed a handful of his shirt up near his right shoulder and yanked hard, ripping off what was left of the sleeve in one smooth stroke. She pressed the improvised bandage into his hand. 'There, maybe now you'll stop considering grass stains to be a big issue.'

Rory slumped to the floor to tend to his wound as Amy slotted her head through a gap between the desk leg and the wardrobe to listen at the door. He grunted as he tugged the bandage tight and began winding it quickly around the bloodied area.

'Is that you?' Amy asked suddenly.

'Is what me?' Rory looked up.

'That smell.'

'What? No!' He paused. 'Wait, what kind of smell?'

Amy wrinkled her nose. 'It smells like…' She mulled the scent over for a second. 'Burning,' she decided finally.

Rory hopped to his feet and strode over to her, quickly grabbing the edge of the wardrobe and tugging it away from the frame by the tiniest of fractions. A sinister grey curl seeped out from under the door.

He ran to the window. 'Blimey. They don't muck about, do they?'

Amy joined him. 'They've set fire to the house. The whole house!'

'Guess it's easier than trying to break in,' Rory muttered.

Spread out across the street in front of them

was a sprawling group of villagers. Orange light flickering across their faces in a manner that reminded Amy of her first bonfire night.

She looked down into the front garden, and saw with little surprise that Isley and the house's occupants were looking up at her, petrol canisters swinging nonchalantly from their hands like so many watering cans. The metal head of the housewife spotted the pair's frightened faces as they looked down at her single eye from their attic room and, with one hand holding her husband's, she reached up another to wave a fond farewell. A few minutes later and all three of their heads were obscured by thick black smoke as it billowed out from the downstairs windows, heralding the red gobs of flame that hissed and crackled their way upwards across the dry wooden cladding of the building towards them.

Chapter
9

Washington DC, 28 February 1981

The inquiry hearing lasted six hours and thirty-seven minutes and Albert and Geoff sat quietly on the front bench as the independent tribunal heard the multitude of testimonies that were brought forward. Their faces displayed no emotion when the room was dimmed and the slides were projected onto the back wall of the courtroom. With each new photograph of each new body, they remained silent, staring impassively into the middle distance. Eventually the judge could bear it no longer and, following an impressive speech regarding the lack of respect for human life displayed by certain people in certain sectors of the military, she adjourned the hearing.

Albert hauled himself painfully out of his tight wooden seat, shaking the cramp from his legs, and Geoff patted a comforting hand on his shoulder as he stood to join him. Together, the pair walked resolutely from the courtroom, heads held high, their eyes refusing to meet the gaze of the crowd.

The ornately carved wooden doors slammed ominously behind them, breaking the silence and sparking a flurry of chatter from the courtroom inside. An angry hubbub of dissatisfaction and protest – the tribunal wanted their heads.

Both men turned quickly down a side corridor that opened into a small, glass-walled courtyard at the centre of the Halls of Justice and swore simultaneously.

'Well that was a bit of a mess,' Geoff growled.

Albert snorted with derision. 'Yes, Geoff, yes it was a bit of a mess. A bit of a mess that we could have avoided if you hadn't pushed the project into a dry run without proper analysis of the combat programming.'

'Oh, what, so it's *my* fault they slashed the budget?' Geoff gestured to himself sarcastically. 'I'm sorry, I thought I could trust the man whose *job* it was to program the damned thing, the man who *claimed* it would work because he was so insanely brilliant.'

Albert began pacing up and down the courtyard, the flagstones creating a circular path for him as he kicked at the bordering plants that hung limply out of their flowerbeds.

'It was programmed to destroy anyone who was aware that it was an android – that's what you wanted! What's a few civilian casualties here and there, when your precious US military technology needs to be kept top secret?'

'Fifty corpses isn't a "few here and there", it's a massacre! God knows how they're going to square this with Cuba.'

'Oh yeah, and you'd know about that wouldn't you? How many innocent civilians became collateral damage on your watch? Or is Vietnam different somehow?'

There was silence for a second, and Albert realised he'd gone too far. His fears were quickly confirmed as he found himself violently shoved backwards and pinned to the glass window that looked out onto the courtyard with the full force of the colonel's strength. The window cracked.

'Don't you *dare* bring up Vietnam.' Geoff was so filled with rage that his voice faded to a harsh whisper. 'You have no idea of the things I've seen, the things I had to do, the things that were done to me and my men. Sitting in your ivory tower with your pet projects – no wonder you've lost perspective. That is if you ever had any.'

It took all of Albert's strength to push the soldier off, and when he next spoke his anger matched the colonel's. 'Oh so that's how it is, is it? That's how you see me?'

Geoff was silent.

'And I suppose we're conveniently forgetting that it's your involvement in *my* work that's keeping you from an enforced retirement package, old soldier? What are you, pushing 50? What exactly would you be without me? What exactly do you think *you* have left to offer the people in there?' He pointed back towards the courtroom, and Geoff found his hard stare unavoidable. 'I've been your virtual prisoner for three years. My existence wiped from the records, my every move monitored; the knowledge in my head a permanent green light for execution if I even *think* about talking to someone. Perspective is not something I have much access to.'

'You didn't seem that fussed when we were writing you a fat paycheque every month,' said Geoff.

'And what was I going to spend it on? My girlfriend? My wife? My kids? I virtually sleep in the workshop so a house was out of the question.'

'There were the inter-departmental singles nights.'

Albert laughed bitterly. 'Oh great, yeah thanks, that's fantastic, cheers, Dad. You might as well pick a girlfriend for me yourself. It's pathetic.'

'As pathetic as *building* your own girlfriend?'

The words hit Albert like a slap in the face, and he faltered for a minute before continuing. 'Isley is the only thing that is mine; her face, her body, her mind are the only aspects of my life that I have control over. You've taken everything else from me, every single thing, and now we can't go back – there's no way out of this! You took my life away six years ago on that beach in California and burned it, and then *this* was my life. This was my life because you gave me nothing else, Geoff – nothing! And now even that's gone now. You might as well have put a bullet through my brain and saved me the effort!' Tears were flying down Albert's cheeks now as he waved his hands about in anger and frustration, his shirt already soaked with sweat.

Geoff just stood there in silence and weathered the abuse until, finally, the scientist dropped to the ground, cradling his head in his hands and sobbing uncontrollably.

'I'm sorry,' was all Geoff could say. He slumped to his haunches and put his arms around Albert's heaving shoulders. 'We'll sort it out. I'll sort it out. I promise.'

Albert slumped back and rested his head against the side wall, looking upwards into the bright rectangle of sky above his head, the evening sun dipping down below the roof arches. He breathed in slowly and exhaled deeply. His eyes were red and raw, but there was still a spark shining dimly amongst the tears.

'So…' Albert breathed again. 'What do we do now?'

Geoff straightened up once more and followed Albert's gaze upwards. He sighed. 'We've been ordered to go and oversee the clean-up operation. They're getting rid of everything, destroying the evidence. Officially the last six years never existed.'

Albert wiped an eye with his palm. 'And how do they intend to do that? We've got fifty operational models in the basement. They're virtually indestructible.'

'Ever heard of Appletown?' Geoff asked.

Albert shook his head. 'Where is it?'

'Colorado. It's an old nuclear testing site; they're giving us the go-ahead for one more nuke. Off the record, of course.'

The scientist cracked a haunted smile then, 'Ha, don't ever let me accuse you of not being thorough.' He ran his fingers through his tousled hair, nowadays almost completely grey. 'But what about the Limited Test Ban treaty? It's not going to be easy covering up a mushroom cloud.'

'President Reagan's administration has decided the Cold War needs some hotting up – no more skulking and stockpiling, it's time to show that we won't be intimidated. The President feels this is a good enough justification to test the boundaries of what the USSR will put up with. We're asking for trouble, deliberately.'

Albert exhaled slowly. 'Jeez.'

Geoff smiled back. 'Jeez indeed.'

Chapter
10

Colorado, 28 August 1981, 3.28 p.m.

The desert had been swept clean across a quarter-mile radius from the edges of Appletown, and the Doctor was glad of his boots as he stepped over the border and into the rough wasteland. Here the rocks were bigger, the ground more uneven and the undisturbed sand held a darker hue than the recently overturned land that made up the foundation of the nuclear test site.

Out in the open, the scorching heat of the sun was heavy and oppressive and the deep blue sky hung dense and low. The Doctor had long since slung his jacket over his shoulder, but the itchy fabric against his back was still making him sweaty and uncomfortable. He unhooked a button on his shirt and shielded his brow to peer into the shimmering blur of the horizon. The ground rippled like water, but he was sure that the darker streaks of a building were beginning to appear in the golden haze.

Spurred on by this encouraging brown smudge, the Doctor resumed his saunter, whistling a jaunty tune and watching in mild wonder as small fragments of gravel bounced along the ground toward his boots with each step that he took.

Then time stuttered once more.

The Doctor yelled in agony as every molecule in his body was shunted forwards half a metre without any intermediate shift, and he choked on air that was suddenly being sucked into his mouth rather than exhaled. He doubled over in pain, stumbling backwards as his boots scuffed the coarse ground.

Another shift, gentler this time, and the Doctor's personal time was restored to its anti-clockwise progression. He placed a hand on his tender stomach. Things were only going to get worse as he continued – the more he interacted with the world around him, the more the universe would protest. But he didn't have a choice.

He resumed his walk once more, moving briskly to hide the shake in his legs, from himself more than anything. The horizon maintained its constant line as the minutes ticked inexorably away, and the Doctor found himself wishing for the slope of a distant mountain range to slide into view, something to show that he was making progress.

He glanced over his shoulder. Appletown was no more than a reflected cascade of sunlight behind him, and in the dead silence of the desert he began to feel rather lonely.

He found a boulder further along, and unceremoniously dumped his jacket on it before slumping onto its vaguely horizontal surface. He reached down to retrieve a spray of brush that had been snapped off its parent stalk. It was black and ashy, reforming into a more organic-looking composition as he rubbed his fingers along the stalk. He moved to put it in his mouth and have a chew and then thought better of it. He fumbled in the inner pocket of his jacket and whipped out the sonic screwdriver.

The familiar crackle of its Geiger setting made him gingerly return it to the ground, the stalk reattaching to the bush as he moved it closer. Fascinating. If he could already see the effects of his actions before he caused them, did that mean that he was obliged to follow a particular course? For these moments, moving backwards through a universe of progression, was every minute detail of his life mapped out before him? He rubbed his chin and shivered at the implications, then patted the thick cotton of his jeans with a loud series of slaps as if announcing a change in mood.

He turned back in what he was sure was the direction he had been walking in and opened his mouth in surprise. Whilst he had been ruminating, three dark green dots had appeared on the horizon, and now they were steadily growing larger before his eager eyes. The dots became blurs, and the blurs became rectangles, and soon the atmospheric haze retreated to reveal three large, camo-painted army trucks thundering in the Doctor's direction.

'Civilisation!' The Doctor grinned.

But his face fell as the trucks approached, reversing towards him at high speed. Their rear hatches were cracked and broken, hinges dented and deformed like the rest of the vehicle by a spattering of bullet holes that covered their back ends.

The Doctor's hair spread across his face in the gust that accompanied the vehicles as they sped past him in the direction of Appletown, the unfastened ends of their covering tarpaulins snapping and cracking along the metal side panels. The soldiers in the cabins looked at him wearily as they drew alongside – a tired sadness like they were too exhausted to care but thought they should at least pretend. The Doctor rubbed his nose and hoped that the dark brown stains that streaked the green paintwork of the trucks were only rust, then turned and continued on his way. He had no desire to return to Appletown just yet.

It was half an hour later when the Doctor checked his watch once more, hopping awkwardly from foot to foot in an attempt to gauge the length of his shadow against the position of the sun against the hands that ticked across the gold-plated timepiece.

Roughly he jammed his thumb into the air, blotting out the sun, and felt some consolation in the discovery that his personal time line was running neither faster nor slower than the world around him; a perfect negative progression. The Doctor wasn't entirely sure whether that was a positive thing or not.

He checked behind himself, and a smile spread across his face as he spotted the familiar shimmer of the trucks returning from their excursion to the town. 'About time!' he shouted, 'I was getting lonely. Now, how about a lift?'

Dark eyes fixed firmly on the reversing convoy he began sidestepping swiftly from side to side, trying to line himself up with the approaching vehicles. His gaze alighted on a faint set of tyre marks a few metres to his right and, with a hop and a step, he planted himself firmly between the tracks. Triumphantly he raised his arms and began gesticulating wildly in an attempt to alert one of the drivers to his presence.

The trucks roared ever closer and the Doctor began to splutter as engine fumes coalesced out of the atmosphere around him, dust blowing away from the markings on either side defining the tracks as they approached. But still they made no sign of acknowledgement, continuing to approach at considerable speed.

His face fell. 'Middle of the desert, in a hurry, weapons testing site, and the fact that to them I must appear to be waving goodbye…' The right-hand vehicle was almost upon him now, a rapidly diminishing gap of only a few metres. 'Not exactly the kind of situation where you'd need to check your mirrors!'

He leapt into the air as high as he could as the clanking back panel of the truck slammed into him, long fingers grasping for a handhold on the camo-painted wood. He hooked his elbows over the edge and hung on for dear life as his boots kicked dangerously close to the rocky ground that was now hurtling past beneath his feet.

There was a rough jolt as one of the wheels glanced a particularly large boulder and the Doctor found himself flipped into the rear of the truck, his stomach catching the panel as he toppled into the shadow of the covered compartment, winding him. It took several empty gasps for his lungs to kick back into action and he gulped in great mouthfuls of stale air as he rolled slowly onto his back and cradled his head in his hands.

Eventually he opened his eyes and immediately wished he hadn't. So he closed them again.

Cautiously, he reopened one eye.

Standing over him, impossibly still, swaying gently with the motion of the truck, were seventeen citizens of Appletown, and in his direct line of sight was Mr Sanderson.

The truck lurched again and the Doctor slid across the floor, grabbing the man's pinstriped trouser leg to halt himself. It felt warm and soft to the touch – too human for comfort – and he snapped his hand away quickly, wiping it on his jacket as he swayed slowly to his feet.

His face drew level with the man he would dismantle nearly two hours from now. 'Yeah,' he muttered, half to himself and half to the impassive figure. He jutted his jaw and stared into the grey-green gel-eyeballs as they blinked gently. 'Sorry about that,' he finished.

Absently, he lifted his hand to his neck and began to scratch. Then he stuck a couple of fingers down his collar and rubbed down his collarbone, and his other hand soon joined it as the Doctor began to scratch himself all over.

'Urgh!' he declared. 'I'm all itchy!' With a concerted effort he stopped scratching and drew his fringe away from his face. 'Why am I itchy? I'm not usually itchy, am I? I'm far too busy to worry about being itchy all the time.' He spread his palms, then flipped them face down in front of him and began to rotate slowly, watching intently as the hairs on the backs of his hands lifted gently and moved ever so slightly. He stopped as he turned to face the rear of the truck. 'An electromagnetic field,' he murmured.

He strode over to the back wall of the driver's cabin and yanked open a metal hatch. Inside was a large coil of metal wrapped around a series of blinking tubes that lined a large iron core.

The Doctor screwed up his face as the itchiness increased even further and whistled through his teeth. 'Phew, that's one serious bit of kit for the eighties.' He turned to the nearest figure. 'You're an expensive lot to maintain, aren't you? Don't you know there's a recession on?'

The figure snapped its hand up and slapped the Doctor's hand away from the panel in an awkward motion. The Doctor ducked out of instinct, yelping in pain as he knocked the open hatch closed to avoid the second blow. But the blow didn't come. The Doctor squinted into the shadow at the sunken face that looked back at him. 'Hold on a minute.' The sonic appeared in his hand, emitting a sharp burst of emerald light. 'You're not an android.' He flipped the device in his hand and examined the catch. 'You're one hundred per cent human being! Why are you in a truck full of killer robots?' He paused for a second. 'Hold on, why am *I* in a truck full of killer robots?' He shook the thought from his head and refocused his attentions on the human.

The man stared at him blankly before uttering a string of incomprehensible syllables and slumping back onto the wooden plank that stood in for a seat along the edges of the truck.

The tarpaulin covering of the vehicle flapped loosely at the edges, and the Doctor examined the figure in the brief shards of sunlight. Grey hair, grey eyes, a dirty brown tie that matched a dirty brown-checked shirt, crumpled beneath a grimy lab coat that must surely once have been white. This man had been through hell.

Realisation dawned slowly on the Doctor, as the previous exchange between his companions flooded his mind. Albert.

'Oh,' he said slowly. 'Oh dear.'

He stood there for a minute, unsure what to do. Without any means to communicate he was at a loss, but Albert looked at him with a mournful familiarity that made the Doctor assume he might come to know him better. He certainly hoped so.

'All right, budge up, then.' The Doctor shoved his hands in his jacket pockets as he slid the man across the bench so that he could sit down. 'Oof, that's better.' He wiggled his boots out in front of him. He hadn't realised just how cramped his feet had become during the long walk. He turned to his companion. 'Right. Er… Right,' he finished limply.

He let the motion of the truck wash over them for a while, gently rocking from side to side and watching as the grey shapes of buildings dawned on the horizon through the open rear of the truck, like a film in a darkened movie theatre. Finally, he decided he could stand the tension no more.

'Oh, c'mere!' he said to the scientist, wrapping his arm around the man's thin shoulders and hugging him tightly to him. 'Thanks. Thanks for helping my friends escape. If you did. I'm sure you did.' He choked and looked at Albert with eyes that were tired of looking at death and turning away. 'And thanks for being here, so that I could tell you that.'

There was a grinding squeal and the Doctor broke away from the scientist, turning to discover that the truck had halted. Huge corrugated iron doors loomed ahead, blotting out the light, and he realised that they had arrived at the military outpost.

The gates began to shudder, the noise swiftly drawing into a loud clang and they began to swing rapidly open at the hands of a group of soldiers who began chaining them to hastily erected posts. The Doctor could hear the accompanying trucks reversing into position around him, and he pushed carefully through the static bodies until he reached the wooden panelling at the rear of his own vehicle. A swift hop and he was over the side, crunching to the ground with ease.

In response, the soldiers lazily drew their weapons up to their faces, aiming at the Doctor down the barrel of a series of large and intimidating rifles.

'Oh dear,' said the Doctor. 'What will I do now?'

He was cut off by what he assumed was the loud barking of orders, no doubt to enter the truck he had just exited.

'Yes, yes. I complied, I went quietly, no problemo, relax.'

He walked forward, into the shadow of the

compound, keen eyes examining the handful of men who backed away in front of him, guns still trained, and he realised that they were shaking.

'I have a very bad feeling about this.'

The Doctor pulled his jacket tighter. Something at the back of his mind was beginning to panic about the dust and grime that had started to coat the tweed as he patted the material down. He ignored the clanging from behind him as another squad of soldiers began to unload the cargo from the truck; docile citizens lined up and were carefully unticked from a checklist. The vista in front of him was much more terrifying.

As they edged backwards, in time with his steps, the Doctor could see that his guards were seriously injured. One of them could barely walk, staggering whenever weight was applied to his right foot, dark patches on his torn trouser leg, flapping over a seeping bullet wound.

The man in the centre was no better off; slowly unwrapping a bandage from around his head. And the other soldiers, their faces blackened and bruised, their uniforms crumpled and torn; all of them had suffered horrendously.

The Doctor refocused his gaze to his surroundings, dreading what he knew was coming into focus as his eyes adjusted to the low light.

Sprawled all over the compound, great pools

of crimson soaking the sandy ground around them, were the bodies of over three dozen dead soldiers.

Chapter

11

Colorado, 28 August 1981, 2.00 p.m.

'Yes, yes. No, sir. We're working as fast as we can.' Geoff screwed up his face in frustration at the tiny voice of authority that crackled through the speaker of a huge plastic mobile phone he had awkwardly stuck between his shoulder and his ear. In one hand he held a very large wad of papers bound in a pale blue folder with a biro jammed between two of his fingers, while his free hand scratched idly at the balding pate beneath his itching official hat.

'Look, sir, speaking freely for a moment, it frankly doesn't make a difference what's going on over there; it's impossible to move any quicker than we're already doing. The paint's still drying on the houses for God's sake, and we can't afford enough electromagnetic emitters to move the androids any quicker without risking a trigger. There are too many dead zones they have to pass through as it is, and we have no idea if the village will actually work.'

He scratched one last time then tore the cap off in frustration, hurling it at the thick glass of the observation window. There was a soft bang and it ricocheted onto the large foldout table that was pushed up against the wall. Pinned roughly to the unvarnished tabletop was a large map, the majority of which was almost completely blank – there was just a large red felt-tipped 'X' scrawled in the middle of it, surrounded by a village plan printed in faint blue rectangles. Even the grey contour lines of the tediously flat landscape seemed half-hearted, taking a back seat to the compass lines and trajectory maps that had been imposed precisely and brutally over the top.

Geoff slapped his folder roughly onto the map and, with a swift movement of his knuckles, brought the biro into his thumb and forefinger to write a humourless *You are here* in the lower corner of the diagram.

'No, no,' he continued into the phone. 'There *were* the funds. You just didn't want to allocate them to a project that was terminating.' Another pause. 'I am fully aware of how much a nuke costs, but that wasn't my decision, so you can either have this done quickly or you can have it done safely. I don't need to remind you of the security risks involved if it goes wrong.'

The voice on the other end of the phone increased in volume, and Geoff winced, hurriedly reaching up and pulling the handset away from his ear.

'These are my men, sir! I'm not going to put their lives in any more danger than I have to!'

A lower, more threatening tone accompanied the response.

'Yes, well, a lot of things will probably happen after this is over, but they *are* my men for now, and until I am relieved of the responsibility I will do it my way. Yes, sir. Goodbye.'

There was a dull thud as the mobile was slammed down onto the table, closely followed by Geoff's elbows as he slumped into his chair and sunk his head in his hands. The folder was jammed underneath his left arm and he elbowed the wad of papers onto the floor to clear himself some space. He hadn't eaten all day, but his stomach was now too painful for him to even consider filling it.

He rocked backwards, pushing his palms up and over his face into his hair and playing with the wispy strands over his bald spot once more. His ashen face was bathed a warm orange by the daylight from outside, tinted through the safety glass. The sun might have been hidden by the slanted corrugated roof that overhung the view, but he could still feel its warmth in the claustrophobic atmosphere of the room.

The observation tower stood three storeys high, tall enough to look out over the huge, barbed-wire-topped walls that marked the boundaries of the compound. The desert glow beyond resembled a sickly orange fog and Geoff screwed up his face in disgust.

Without looking, he reached down to his belt and unclipped his walkie-talkie, turning his head slightly to speak into the grated microphone. 'Albert, I don't care what you're doing, I want you up here now!'

There was a crackle, then a response. 'What's the problem?'

'Don't ask what the problem is, just get up here and I'll tell—'

Geoff's attention was diverted once again by the view through the glass. Was that a man on a bicycle riding into the desert? He shook his head and looked again.

'Hello? You broke off?'

Geoff blinked and it was gone. 'Too twitchy,' he

growled. 'Gotta stop doing this.' He thumbed the button again. 'Just get up here.'

'Lord. This is a bit dramatic, isn't it?'

Geoff spun around at the sound of Albert's voice as the scientist gestured to the orange observation glass.

'It's to stop us going blind,' he responded.

Albert nodded slowly. 'Does it stop us getting cancer, too?'

Geoff gave a harsh laugh. 'Cancer's too long-term for the government to take the blame. They'll no doubt tell us it's our diet when we're all on life support in ten years.'

Albert yanked a half-eaten sandwich from his pocket and took a large bite. 'What's the deal then?' he asked between chews. 'Is the mood lighting making you feel all urgent again?'

'Yeah, you won't be joking after you hear this.'

'Ruin my day.'

'There's a Russian spy plane just passed over the west coast, heading our way. They've obviously heard something's going on.'

'I thought that was the point.' Albert took another mouthful.

'Yeah, well let's not even start on the political mess we've been stuck in the middle of. They were meant to arrive after the nuke went off. Now they're early, so Command wants us to get a move on.'

Albert didn't look as agitated as Geoff had hoped. 'Did you tell them it's not like we've been sitting around here doing nothing all morning?'

Geoff didn't reply, instead flicking his gaze to the scientist's sandwich and back. He raised an eyebrow.

'What? I'm not meant to be doing everything myself! Things don't stop just because I have something to eat.'

'I didn't say anything.'

'You didn't need to.' He went to toss the crust into a bin. 'I'm not hungry now, anyway.'

'Whatever.' Geoff reached for the radio again. 'I'm telling the men to start putting the androids on the trucks.'

Albert's face fell for a second, and he quickly disguised his look of dismay with a cough and a fumble in his pockets. He brought out a pen and clicked it a few times before realising that there was nothing for him to do with it and put it away again. 'Er, really? Now?' He choked for a second.

Geoff looked at him suspiciously. 'Yes. That's not going to be a problem is it?'

'I just… I just had some things I wanted to do.' Albert thought of something suddenly. 'Besides the EM field hasn't been set up in the courtyard.'

'They've been in the transport fields long enough; it'll take them at least half an hour to come out of reset – plenty of time to load the trucks. Just make sure the soldiers don't say anything stupid.' He paused, reluctant to talk budgets with Albert. 'You do know that the EM generators cost about three times as much as the village? At least this way we'll be able to scrape a few nickels back on the parts if we don't set them up. To be completely frank with you, we need the brownie points with command. Our futures aren't looking good.'

Albert opened his mouth as if to protest, but decided against it. He nodded sullenly.

Geoff turned back to the radio. 'Action stations. Action stations. All personnel to the courtyard. We're going to load the trucks. Watch your mouths out there – there's no EM field, so the less the androids hear, the more likely it'll be that we all live through this.'

A scattering of 'Yes, sir' responses came crackling back, and the colonel returned his attention to the scientist who stood hunched in his lab coat by the door.

'You will tell me if there's something wrong,' Geoff said, his voice hinting at a softer undertone. 'This operation is too delicate to have you going rogue on me.'

Albert smiled. 'Oh I'm not going anywhere.'

Suddenly the walkie-talkie screeched once more, and Geoff rolled his eyes. 'Is there a problem, Post Five?' he snapped. 'Need a diagram?'

'Uh, no, sir,' the timid sergeant responded. 'Just thought I'd inform you that we have a houseguest.'

Geoff looked puzzled. 'A houseguest?'

'Yes sir. Seems to have come from Apple- er, I mean the village.'

There was a pause.

'On a bicycle,' the sergeant finished sheepishly.

The relief Geoff felt for discovering that he wasn't hallucinating was overshadowed by the surprise Geoff felt for discovering that he wasn't hallucinating. 'A bicycle?' he echoed.

'Yes, sir. And that's not the only strange thing about him, sir.'

'Surprise me.'

'I think he's foreign. He can't speak properly and he walks all... funny.'

Geoff sighed. 'He sounds like the worst spy I've ever heard of.'

'But he's not a spy, sir.'

'No?'

'He has an American Health and Safety Pass – Access All Areas.'

'Sergeant, such a thing doesn't even exist. Who

ever heard of a Health and Safety officer with complete military clearance? You know what? Don't answer that. Just bring him up.' Geoff released his thumb from the call button angrily and dropped the walkie-talkie into a nearby paper bin. It rattled satisfyingly in the tin container. 'I am surrounded by idiots,' he said, almost sadly.

Albert was silent, and Geoff turned to look at him with such sadness in his eyes that the scientist thought he was going to cry.

'What have we done?' said Geoff.

'I don't know.'

'You know this means war, once the Russians spot the nuke.'

'I know.'

Geoff welled up then stifled it quickly, sleeve across his face before emitting an exhausted laugh. 'Not much use for infiltration androids anyway, I guess, in that case.'

Albert laughed in sympathy. 'No, I guess not. But at least our part will be over when this is done.'

'Do you think it'll stay with us?'

'What?'

'The fact that we were here at the start. Do you think we'll be able to forgive ourselves?'

Albert turned away, moving to look out of the window. 'I never had a choice.'

Geoff didn't respond and after a few seconds he dropped to his haunches with an exasperated groan and began gathering the papers that had spilled out of his blue folder. From the middle of the file a particular sheet slipped out and zigzagged away across the floor. He reached out to grab it and, as he turned the sheet over, he noticed that something had been written on it. Scrawled roughly in chunky red felt-tip, the message read *I am living backwards through time. There is no point asking me any more questions.* There was a gap then of a few lines before one final phrase. *I'm sorry.*

'Strange,' Geoff muttered.

'What is?' Albert looked around. The colonel flipped the sheet over in his hand but the rear was covered merely in the same inscrutable typeface that the other small-print sections of his folder contained. The scientist peered over his shoulder.

'A joke?'

'Maybe, but this folder came straight to my hands from the Pentagon. There were no intermediaries.'

'Maybe it's a test to see if you actually read the whole thing. If it is, I don't think you've passed.'

Geoff placed the sheet carefully on the foldout table. 'Ridiculous.'

Albert began shifting restlessly. 'OK, well, if that's everything, Geoff, I think I'd better get downstairs to do some overseeing.' He moved towards the door.

'No, wait,' Geoff called after him. 'There is one more thing.'

He moved over to a stark grey filing cabinet and pulled out a bunch of keys, Albert watching him intently as he fiddled, painfully slowly, through the collection for the correct one. The drawer finally open, Geoff reached inside and pulled out a parcel wrapped in browning Christmas wrapping paper. 'Sorry,' he said apologetically. 'It was the only paper left in the house.'

He hefted it in his grip and Albert extended a hand to take it, but Geoff didn't move. 'It's sort of a... goodbye gift, y'see,' he began. 'Probably shouldn't give it to you now, but it seemed appropriate given the circum—'

A loud bang cut him off, and the door to the observation deck slammed open, nearly striking the scientist in the back as he hopped out of the way. Geoff hurriedly pushed the package back into the drawer and slid it closed. 'What... what is the meaning of this?' he stammered guiltily. 'You can't just barge into a confidential meeting!'

'Sorry, sir.'

It was the nervous sergeant. Geoff didn't know his name, nor had he any wish to. He knew the men on the base weren't really working for him;

there was a greater agenda from a higher authority driving their actions. 'We've brought you the, ah, Health and Safety guy.'

Albert raised an eyebrow as a tall young man hopped backwards into the room with astounding grace for someone who couldn't see where he was going. Bow tie, drainpipes, tweed jacket, fancy hair – he would have blended in well in the hipper areas of Michigan, but as a Health and Safety government official he looked frankly ludicrous.

The man turned to spot the pair, waving a swift hello accompanied by the strangest sound the scientist and the colonel had ever heard.

'Yibtoog. Yeerrur yah nee meiy,' the man intoned solemnly.

Albert looked at Geoff. Geoff looked at Albert.

'Anything?'

'Nope.'

The scientist shoved his hands into his pockets and slipped around behind the sergeant and his two guards. He grinned over their heads. 'Well, good luck with that, then. I'll leave you to it!'

'Wait, where are you going?'

Albert considered lying, but he was in a hurry. 'I've got my own goodbyes to make,' he said, before closing the door behind him.

Geoff didn't have time to respond. He turned to find the strange man standing over by the map on his table. 'What the hell do you think you're doing?' he growled, stepping over to haul the man away. But when he realised what the stranger was doing he stopped in his tracks, hand resting on the nearby chair.

The man had picked up the sheet of paper. He inspected it thoroughly for a few moments before carefully taking the red felt-tip from the far corner of the table and beginning to trace over the message scrawled on the back.

Geoff raised his eyebrows in shock as the writing began to vanish with each stroke of the pen. A moment later and the paper was blank, the felt-tip clattering to the lino floor. The man turned to point at him, then at the backs of his knees, a comical look of surprise on his face. He motioned to the chair. 'Ewe tat zow?' he said.

'I am so not in the mood for this.' Geoff closed his eyes in anger. 'What's that, Mr Crazy?' he said, mimicking the Doctor's gesture. 'You want the chair?' He heaved it swiftly and violently. 'Well, take a seat why don't you?' The chair slammed across the room into the man as he spun around. The plastic seat hit his legs and he dropped suddenly and unexpectedly onto the seat, his face screwed up in pain. The soldiers standing at the back of the room exchanged glances, but the sergeant shook his head.

'He's in control,' he said.

'– sednoo dnoad eye,' the man started shouting mid-sentence. His voice was tinged with frustration and sadness.

Geoff began pacing up and down in front of the prisoner. 'I haven't got time for this, Mr Crazy,' he snarled. 'So stop with the gobbledegook and start talking.'

There was no response.

'Who's side are you on?' he yelled.

Still nothing.

'What are you doing here? Where are you from?'

The stranger looked up at him impassively and shrugged. Geoff broke.

'Where are you from? Where are you from? Where are you from? Where are you from?!' Each demand brought his face an inch closer to the man until he could see flecks of his own spit on his prisoner's cheeks.

The man slowly raised a hand and reached into the inside of his jacket pocket to withdraw a thin leather wallet. He flipped it open. 'Won?' he said.

'Health and Safety?' Geoff roared. 'Do you have any idea what's going on here?' He drew back a clenched fist, but the clack of the sergeant's boots as he stepped forward, ready to intervene, made him hesitate and rethink.

The man slapped the wallet closed and stuffed it back inside the jacket, raising a finger as he did so with a sharp exclamation of 'won eye'.

'I give up,' Geoff said rubbing the back of his jaw. It ached from his explosion of anger. 'Take him away.'

The sergeant stepped forward, sweat glistening on his top lip. 'Er, where, sir?' he asked. 'Do you want us to let him go?'

'Of course I don't want you to let him go!' Geoff snapped. 'If he's a spy then he knows too much, if he's a US citizen he *definitely* knows too much, and if he's not a US citizen *or* a spy then nobody will care what happens to him. Load him in the trucks with the androids and return him to the village.'

'Are you sure? He'll die! Uh… you know he doesn't exactly seem to be too with it. Sir.'

'Don't question me, soldier.' Geoff spat the last word. He swivelled his head menacingly. 'You've missed the party, sonny. There are too many deaths on my conscience already from this project for me to be swayed by a… freak. Maybe you should think about how much *you* know about the classified nature of the work you're doing here before you start questioning orders.'

The sergeant swallowed.

'Exactly,' Geoff continued. 'This isn't going to end happily, I can tell you that right now. And if *any* of us –' He looked around the room at the other men – 'live to see tomorrow, then I suggest that you head directly to the nearest church, because you'll have been blessed my friends. And it will truly be a miracle.'

'Yes sir,' the sergeant choked, snatching the stranger's proffered hands as he stood up from his chair and hauling him to the exit. The nearest soldier grabbed the handle and yanked the door open.

Suddenly, every man in the room froze.

'What on God's green earth is that?' Geoff whispered hoarsely.

Drifting up from the steel staircase outside the open door was the sound of screaming. There was a sharp burst of gunfire that cut off abruptly, and then suddenly the alarm kicked in, a howling klaxon that made all talk virtually impossible.

The soldiers thrust their palms against their ears, and Geoff had to shout to make himself heard.

'They've been triggered!' he yelled. 'The androids are on the loose!'

Chapter
12

Colorado, 28 August 1981, 2.38 p.m.

Albert closed the door to the observation room as slowly as he felt was necessary to avoid arousing suspicion, and his soft brown loafers barely made a noise as he padded down the rough iron staircase to the outpost below. Even at the bottom he could still hear Geoff's roaring voice, and he smiled wryly to himself, half in sympathy at the poor stranger and half in relief that he wasn't in the same room to suffer the colonel's wrath.

The shanty town of the outpost glistened in the early afternoon sun as he walked through it. He was surprised to see that there were still large groups of men sitting around on the various crates and barrels that were strewn around the dusty walkways between the hastily erected officers' messes, soldiers' messes, sleeping quarters and storerooms.

'Oi oi, chop chop!' He gave a sharp clap with his hands drawing the attention of the stragglers as they turned their heads lazily to look at him. 'No one's waiting for you, so if you don't want to be in the village when the nuke hits I recommend *getting a move on!*'

There were groans and moans as the men eased themselves away from the shady metal walls and into the harsh light, trailing behind the scientist as he strode purposefully towards the unmarked transport trucks that had been walled into the complex.

He paused at a particularly stubborn group who were playing cards on the kegs behind the mess and made a show of peering over the shoulder of the closest man. 'Two aces, boys,' he said cheerfully. 'I'd get out while you still can.'

The men threw down their cards in unison. 'Thanks a lot, sir, I was clearing up!' the lead player protested, quickly grabbing the notes on the table before any other members of the circle had a chance to reclaim their cash.

Albert waved back at them over his shoulder without looking round. 'Don't care!'

His stride was too quick to be casual as he rounded the corner to the parking lot, a tarmac section of road that had been boxed in by the huge imposing walls. The trucks had been positioned at as much of an angle as possible. With their delicate interiors and tyres that were certainly not fit for the rocky terrain off the beaten track, it still meant a lot of awkward manoeuvring of the cargo to take it down the covered interior corridor that led to the main courtyard, and the vans that would transport them on the final leg of the journey.

Foldout steps had been lowered from the backs of the vehicles, and a stifling hush had fallen on the area, a stark contrast to the low chatter Albert had experienced up until now. Silently, the future citizens of Appletown were being guided carefully down and out into the open as if they were the most delicate things imaginable. Only their basic motor functions were active after so many hours of being bathed in the interior EM fields of the trucks. Sweat dripped from every soldier's brow, each of them fully aware that one false move could be his last, and it was with a gentle touch that Albert silently pushed through the flanking guardsmen with their itchy trigger fingers.

He watched intently as his creations were escorted to their deaths. Every one of them, every personality, had been designed and created by him. There was Mr and Mrs Sanderson, the happily married couple, Dave Jones the gardener, that woman in the paisley dress who he'd modelled on his mother – Miranda. The line began to ebb and, as he finished counting the androids off in his head, he knew that there was only one more citizen left to be unloaded.

He tapped the nearby captain on the shoulder. 'I'll take it from here,' he whispered.

The captain looked around sternly, before recognising the scientist. He acknowledged Albert's authority with a curt nod and moved aside.

'By the way, Captain, do you know where my bag is? I think I left it in the driver's cabin. Do you mind fetching it for me?' Albert used his most disarming of smiles. The captain frowned, annoyed at being ordered about by a civilian. 'Now please?' Albert added. Without a word, the captain disappeared around the front of the truck.

The interior of the vehicle was bathed in a soft red glow that made the smooth metal walls feel close and intimidating as Albert walked through the now-empty racks where the androids had been hung for the duration of their transportation. Only one was still occupied, deep in the far corner of the structure where the scientist knew she would be. He grimaced as he gently undid the clasps around her wrists and let her fall softly onto his shoulder.

'There there, Isley,' he whispered. 'Let's get you out of this abattoir.' A gentle pressure on her neck and her motor functions re-engaged, allowing her to stand without support. He took her by the hand, and together they walked out of the lorry and into the harsh sunlight where the captain was waiting impatiently by the steps with Albert's shoulder bag.

Albert nodded appreciatively. 'Cheers.'

The remaining soldiers still stood at attention, flanking either side of the route towards the central courtyard. But rather than follow the escort, Albert ducked to the right, pulling Isley with him. There was a quickly hushed chorus of protests, but the scientist ignored them and fixed his eyes straight ahead as he led the android to a small cluster of barrels in the corner of the car park that semi-obscured the pair from the platoon's condemning eyes.

He sat her on one of the small crates within the semicircle and perched next to her, his long legs making his knees bend awkwardly. 'Do you remember who I am, Isley?' he asked carefully.

The android's head swivelled and turned groggily. 'Hello, Albert,' she said.

Albert's eyes watered. 'That's my girl,' he whispered.

'Do you want to talk to me, Albert?' Isley's intonation circuits had yet to reboot, despite the extra complexities and improvements of a system that had been active for so much longer than all the others. Her voice was flat but feminine and shocked Albert with memories of the computer lab in Michigan over eight years ago.

'Yes, Isley. Yes I do.' He reached for his bag and snapped open the clasp to rummage inside. 'Now, you're about to go on a long journey, sweetie. We're going to take you to a brand new house, built just for you.' He looked around nervously and lowered his voice. 'You remember? Like the one we talked about?'

'The one where you said we could live together and mind our own business as long as everybody else minded theirs.'

A tear rolled down Albert's bristled cheek. 'Yes, exactly, Isley, that's the one. But you're going to have to go there first, on your own, you understand?' He sniffed loudly. 'But I'll see you later. I promise.'

Before the android could respond, Albert's fingers closed around the object in his bag and he smiled through his grief, drawing out a small metal box wired to a pair of headphones. Gingerly, he took Isley's hands and turned them over before ceremoniously placing the Walkman into her open palms.

'Happy fifth birthday, Isley,' he said.

She examined the device impassively. 'My song?' she enquired.

Albert held up his hand. 'Not this time. The Walkman's only half the present – there's a *new* song for you today.' Another rummage in the bag produced a small cassette tape. 'Now be careful with this,' he continued. 'It's my only copy.'

Isley turned the plastic case over in her hand and slipped it into the open slot of the player. She moved to place the earphones over her head as Albert had done with her so many times before. Albert touched her wrists gently before she could do so and carefully rested the earphones back onto her shoulders.

'Not this time,' he said, reaching over to the box and spinning up the volume dial before pressing play.

The tinny power chords of a piano cut through the silence as the scientist stood up and proffered a hand to his companion – an invitation to dance. She took it solemnly.

Hand in hand, the pair walked together into the long undercover walkway of the corridor. Strip lighting flickered erratically above their heads, and the soldiers glared angrily at them from the alcoves between the ribbed supports.

A pair of reinforced double doors swung open in front of them just as the vocals kicked in, and Albert slid one foot forward in an atrocious attempt at a slide whilst making gun-fingers at his partner.

'Just a small town girl. Living in a looonely wooorld!' he sang as they moved through the second gate.

The soldiers guarding the final doors that would open out into the courtyard looked on in astonishment at the sight that confronted them. The ageless young girl in her creator's souvenir *Star Wars* T-shirt, pale jeans and trainers, alongside the greying scientist with his combed-back hair, spectacles and lab coat made such a ridiculous pairing that one of the men couldn't help but grin as they approached. The scientist winked at him as he began an elaborate air guitar display, legs bowed out sideways as he strode forwards, strumming the air, his partner nodding in time.

But the other guard was less impressed. He scowled as he slid the huge bolt across the steel doors and began to haul it open, revealing the large open space beyond, and the mass of cybernetic bodies that were standing there.

Albert and Isley stepped towards the threshold.

'A singer in a smoky room – the smell of wine and cheap perfume!'

'Android lover,' the guard spat.

A second later he fell to the floor, his neck snapped instantly.

Isley withdrew her hand. 'Gotcha,' she said coldly.

Albert had been two steps ahead of her when it happened and turned back in horror, mirroring the action of every single head in the courtyard, android and human alike.

'He said android,' Albert whispered hoarsely, speaking aloud the panicked thought of the surrounding soldiers.

There was a hail of noise as every rifle in the compound was cocked simultaneously and aimed squarely at the suburban mass in the middle of the dusty courtyard. The mass fanned out into a perfect circle, facing their attackers head on.

Nobody moved.

Albert gently edged the door behind him closed as Isley walked out in front of him. It squeaked painfully in the silence.

Suddenly, someone broke. From up above, on the wrought-iron balcony that spanned three-quarters of the courtyard perimeter, a stream of bullets spasmed wildly into the centre of the circle. Clouds of dust pricked up around the android's feet as the bullets buried themselves in the dusty ground.

But the citizens were too fast.

There was a blur of motion that made Albert feel sick and suddenly, without any physical change, the innocuous civilians switched over to their military protocols, transformed instantaneously into killing machines. Corduroy trousers covered piston legs as they pounded into the stomachs of the nearest soldiers, bonded titanium-alloy fists crushing human arms as they tore the weapons from their weakened grip, fingers still randomly twitching at the triggers. Even Isley herself had disarmed the once-grinning guard beside her and stood, feet planted firmly on the ground as she raked the upper level with cold, precise bursts whilst her victim writhed in agony on the floor. Barely a bullet missed its target at the hands of his creations.

Albert stumbled blindly through the panic, hands waving at the air in protest as he begged the robots to stop. The butt of a rifle smacked him in the back of the head and he was sent sprawling across the ground, his body dragged several metres before he regained awareness. Looking upwards and through grit-filled eyes he could see Mr Sanderson standing over him, casually ripping a magazine from the belt of a dead soldier as his body flew past him through the air. There was a soft series of clicks as he reloaded and aimed the barrel squarely at Albert's head.

'No.'

Albert flinched, but the bullet didn't come. He opened his eyes to find Isley standing in the android's place. He looked around, and spotted the man stumbling backwards with some surprise at the force of the shove the young woman had given him. But his microchip brain was not built to bear grudges, and tactical considerations soon took over as he swivelled his head in search of a new target.

With one hand, Isley hauled the prone man into the air, and pushed him into a corner where a small, tarpaulin-covered object had been tucked away. 'Hide,' she stated simply.

Albert cradled his head in his hands, confused more than terrified. 'But why? You're not programmed to save my life. I've known about you, what you are. I built you! I've always known – surely that's all you need to hear!'

Isley paused and tilted her neck. 'I know,' she said. 'But I need you.'

Then she turned away, the muzzle of her rifle flashing almost immediately as she finished off a soldier mid-fall as his body plummeted from the balcony.

Albert reached a hand to his cheek and realised that he was blushing. 'I need you too,' he whispered.

Then the alarms went off.

Chapter

13

Colorado, 28 August 1981, 2.47 p.m.

Geoff cannoned onto the balcony just in time to dodge a hail of bullets that sent him scrambling for cover behind a nearby crate. The nervous sergeant and his prisoner joined him soon after.

'What happened?' He grabbed a pistol off a nearby soldier who was desperately trying to patch up a wound in his arm and fired off a few covering shots.

'It was Dr Gilroy, sir,' the soldier panted through clenched teeth. 'He was... singing or something.'

Geoff blanched. 'Albert did this?' But there was no time to dwell. He turned to his comrade. 'Quick, sergeant. Where's the EM generator?'

'The what, sir?' The sergeant was shaking with fear, jolting as bullets rattled on the underside of the steel floor beneath him.

'The EM generator! You must have been trained to set it up!'

The sergeant pointed directly in front of where they were crouching. 'In the crate, sir.'

That was all Geoff needed. A few well-placed shots, and the padlock disintegrated. He tossed the weapon over to the sergeant and began clawing at the splintered wood, tearing the front panel open. The interior was a mess of wiring and bolts, but the familiar shape of the iron core and its metal spiral were fully intact.

He began fiddling around inside, desperately guessing at which wires needed to be hooked up to which sockets, his calloused fingers unused to such delicate movements. 'How do you switch this thing on?' he growled.

'I don't know, sir.'

'I wasn't looking for an answer, soldier! I could have guessed you wouldn't have a clue!'

The screams of his men below were lessening. There were so few of them left now that even the soft groans of pain were becoming audible. With a howl of exasperation, Geoff stood up and kicked the machine, hard.

It was then that he heard an entirely different

noise altogether: a kind of soft, buzzing sound, like that of a mechanical insect. He turned his head slowly to see the strange man with the strange clothes holding a strange device – a hefty, bronzed tool with an emerald light at one end – which he was pointing at the generator.

'Sabotage!' Geoff mouthed over the noise. He turned quickly, grabbing the stranger and heaving him over the iron railings with a brutal yell of exertion. There was a dull thud as the body hit the ground below, and Geoff braved a glance downwards to inspect the damage. The man had landed awkwardly but the drop hadn't been far enough to injure him in any visible manner. Not that it mattered anyway – the androids were already surrounding his prone figure in preparation for the *coup de grâce*.

Geoff spun around and returned his attention to the crate. It was humming now – the prisoner's device had charged the mechanisms inside, overloading the circuits so that the coil glowed a deep red.

It crackled.

Geoff felt like someone had just handed him a grenade and pulled the pin. His mind flashed back to Vietnam, and he had a sickening feeling of fragility, like his bones were hollow.

Mustering all the strength he could manage, he

heaved the device up and into his arms until it was balanced precariously on the edge of the rail, suddenly overcome with a desire to get the device as far away from himself as possible. He inched it forwards slowly and felt the wood splinter further in his grip.

Below, forty-seven rifles were cocked instantly.

Geoff pushed one last time.

All eyes tracked the trajectory of the crate as it plummeted down into the courtyard. It just missed the stranger and shattered instantly.

Silence.

A smell of burning sawdust drifted lazily through the stifling summer air as the shavings that coated the heap of exposed metal began to smoulder.

Then the generator detonated.

The electromagnetic tsunami that ensued was invisible, but every man in the room could feel it as it radiated out from the ruined device at the speed of light and crashed against the walls of the courtyard with a violence that was expressed only in the suddenly flopping figures of the androids. Like a line of dominos, the future citizens of Appletown stumbled and fell as their programming was brought to an abrupt halt and a state of reset was resumed.

The sound of falling weapons and bodies

pattered around the silent compound like a soft drizzle as Geoff carefully pulled a handkerchief from his pocket and wiped his eyes with a trembling hand.

The massacre was over.

'It was you.'

Time was of the essence, and Geoff had had no time to sympathise with his wounded men as he'd strode into the courtyard, a tight ball of fury, spitting orders in all directions. The survivors were allowed only the most rudimentary of first aid before being set to work, grouping the docile citizens in preparation for the embarkation before they recovered from the shock of the reset.

The huge iron doors to the compound had been opened and, silhouetted against the vast sandscape beyond, the three army trucks hummed reassuringly with the power of their own personal EM fields. A cluster of soldiers gathered around them as they checked off the populace, careful not to stray too far from the dead zone, just in case.

Geoff fixed Albert with a stare that was filled more with disappointment than anger.

'You *killed* my men. Thirty-seven soldiers dead, more wounded, and all because of your feelings for *her*. Because you couldn't keep it professional. Yet again!' He spat as he pointed at the young woman in the battered T-shirt as she was loaded into a vehicle. 'For God's sake, Albert, she's just a, a, a *thing*!' he finished pathetically. He drew a palm over his face and composed himself. 'You got too close. You were always too close. To me *and* to the project. I should have made you shut her down the minute you started implementing those "improvements" over the other models.'

Albert opened his mouth to respond, but Geoff waved him into silence.

'I don't care what you have to say. This is it, it's over, and this is goodbye. Just get on the truck.' He turned away so that Albert couldn't see the tears in his eyes and looked over his shoulder. 'Guards? Take it from here, will you?' His gaze alighted on the prisoner. 'And put that freak in with him.' He gestured. 'They can keep each other company until the nuke goes off.'

The sergeant stepped forward and took Albert by the shoulder. 'Sir?' he said.

'Yeah, let's go,' Albert muttered. He turned and began walking towards the central vehicle.

Every soldier in the compound stopped to watch him board. Every solder staring at him with hollow, condemning eyes that made Albert shrink in his coat as he shuffled to the back of the van. And every soldier was certain in their heads that this was the punishment the scientist deserved.

Every soldier, except Geoffrey Redvers.

By the time Geoff had finished with the observation room it had been almost completely destroyed, and the broken man sat huddled amongst the splintered wreckage of the foldout table, walled in by upturned cabinets, nursing his bruised hands and weeping like a child.

Blinded by tears, he reached out and began scrabbling through the papers and folders that littered the room on his hands and knees until he found what he was looking for: the parcel, in its brown Christmas wrapping paper, torn and peeling away at the edges. He clutched it to his chest and squeezed.

There was a loud rip and the contents spilled into his lap. A shower of bills, travellers' cheques, a passport and other strange items were sent spinning across the room by his crudely kicking feet. The passport hit the wall and fell open on the rear page just as Geoff wiped his eyes on his sleeve in an attempt to calm his heaving shoulders. Groggily, he stumbled to his feet and walked over, his thick fingers reaching down to pick it up. He stood looking at it for a few minutes, running his thumb over the tiny photograph of Albert. The passport had a different name and with it the chance of a different life.

The promise he'd made to try and sort things out.

All gone now.

He folded the little navy book back into his pocket and blew his nose loudly into his handkerchief, turning once more towards the tinted glass to watch the golden sun as it moved steadily across an orange sky.

Then time stopped.

Fell apart.

Was rewritten.

Chapter
14

Colorado, 28 August 1981, 2.41 p.m.

The Doctor stood in the centre of the courtyard, his head snapping this way and that. His riding companion had been unloaded and stood, head hung low as a colonel spoke to him in an even lower timbre of hushed nonsense. The Doctor's guards had long since abandoned him and retreated to the borders of the compound, in the shadows beneath the large balcony, to steadily undress their wounds. The blood on their bandages seemed to evaporate as they steadily unravelled and folded the white cotton into small tin cases.

The Doctor didn't know what to do, and the steadily increasing pain in his chest was beginning to distract him from his train of thought. He walked over to one of the bodies, out of the way of the precisely lined regiments the unloaded citizens of Appletown had been organised into. 'Those things must be quick, impossibly quick,' he muttered. 'There's not a scratch on them.'

Kneeling down he idly placed two fingers on the soldier's neck, feeling for a pulse, but there was none. He counted the corpses.

'Thirty-seven,' he whispered. His voice soon rose to an anguished shout as the impact of what he was about to have to witness became more and more profound. 'This can't happen, how could this happen? I don't want to have to see this. Please!'

As if in response to his cry, the Doctor's fingers twitched and he looked down at the young man's face. Where before there had been nothing but cold skin, there now appeared warmth and the faintest of pulses began to tickle at his fingertips. The ground around his knees became dry and coarse once again as the wounds on his legs closed, and the Doctor looked around nervously. 'It's about to start.'

As he stood up once more he realised that the soldiers had almost finished laying the androids out in a complex pattern around the courtyard, a broken fan, radiating out from a central point. The Doctor ran over to it, his keen mind taking in every detail of the scene and the one person out of place – Albert, now hunched in a corner, beside a tarpaulin. Sharp exhalations of breath began to chorus around him and his walk sped up to a run as all around him the soldiers began to ignite with tiny sparks of life.

A broken crate was lying in pieces just outside of the shadow of the balcony, and he dropped to his knees to investigate it, nearly losing his balance as the stabbing pain intensified. His palms and wrists were aching like hell. Through gritted teeth he examined the debris. 'An EM generator. They can't have activated it in time... How was nobody prepared for this? Why wasn't it already operational?'

He looked up at the railing above him. The colonel who had been overseeing the unloading now rested his elbows on the metal bar of the first floor and looked back at him with cold, steel eyes. A man who had lost everything.

'No,' said the Doctor, lifting his head and railing against the sky. 'It doesn't have to end like this. Just because I've seen the future doesn't mean that's how it has to be! I change things all the time! My actions, anybody's actions, can divert the course of history, how can it matter which direction I approach it – there can't be only one outcome, there *musn't*!'

The pain in his chest was almost unbearable now and it took the entire force of his will not to fall to the ground. But there was another sensation building now, a familiar, tingling sensation on the backs of his hands – an itching.

Behind him, an android twitched. The electromagnetic flash was echoing now, intensifying, focusing into a tight wave of energy that was hurtling into the crate. Splinters of wood, nails, bits of wire zipped past his face as they slammed into the slowly reforming box. The final bullet fired returned to the barrel of its gun with a loud crack.

'No!' the Doctor screamed once more. 'This can't be how it ends!'

Then, suddenly, as if in reply, time stuttered once more.

And the Doctor could see it all.

Frozen, in the final second of the massacre, bullets and blood and bodies suspended in space, dying screams silent in their throats, the Doctor could see everything.

The great white path of the future, the one he had been travelling along all this time, the path of least resistance, the future in which the Time Lord had interacted the least. It burned his mind like a bulldozer, the force of time, desperately trying to flatten the effects of that one man who had dared to contradict the laws of cause and effect, to make him tiny and insignificant in a universe where action always *must* precede reaction, because this was the way it should have been had he never arrived – and in this version the Doctor was relegated to the position of observer only.

But it wasn't the only way. And mere observation was definitely not the Doctor's style.

He might have been blinded by it if he hadn't been so outraged. But now he concentrated and focused and fought the feeling that his head was going to explode until finally he managed to dim the blazing light in his brain, lowering the brightness that made everything else seem unreal and insubstantial. With the greatest of efforts he spotted the tiny, hair-thin paths that blossomed and branched off that central path like strands of a web, billowing and splitting in a breeze of dynamic interaction. The paths of the alternative, the futures he could have travelled if only he'd done something. There was still time.

He took a deep breath, checked his watch and stepped out onto a strand.

The frozen moment skipped forwards and reversed. And the Doctor screamed in agony as every cell in his body was reconfigured into sync with the flow of the universe. He collapsed to his knees and crawled agonisingly across the open space of the courtyard as the sound of dying erupted all around, deafening him. He rolled out of the way of the stomping boot of a soldier as the man made a dash for the exit, only to be cut down metres before he reached the iron gates. The Doctor looked at his watch. 'Three minutes? That's it? Three minutes into the past? I'll revert back before I can do anything! I need something bigger, something more drastic, something big and annoying and against the laws of physics. I need half an hour at least!'

Then he remembered: the person out of place. He scanned the courtyard, dodging his head between the moving bodies, android and human alike until he could see Albert, still in his corner, still huddled against the tarpaulin. He mustered his strength and began to drag himself forward.

There were now only two minutes left before he reached the point at which he had crossed over. Two minutes left before he resumed his backwards journeying from the beginning of the loop. He reached out a trembling hand to the scientist and Albert grabbed it in sympathy, pulling him the last short distance into shelter.

'Are you OK?' Albert asked. 'That was quite a fall.'

'No time for chit chat,' the Doctor panted back.

'You need to tell me now – what happened? Why did this start? What caused it?'

Albert tried to turn away, but the Doctor grabbed his face and turned it back until he was staring deep into the man's terrified eyes.

'I said there was no time! Now tell me!'

'It… it was me,' Albert stuttered. 'I did it, I walked with Isley to the dead zone and someone shouted something. I shouldn't have done it, but I wanted to see her one last time while she was conscious. I love her!'

The Doctor released his grip and laughed desperately. 'That's it, that's all I needed to know.' He looked at his watch. 'And thirty seconds to spare!'

He began to back away, moving over to the landing site of the crate, now being lifted down in the balcony above by the colonel. He snapped his head around quickly. 'I just need something to make sure I'm in sync for that moment. I need to find out what's going to happen next and change it, boot myself into the past even further to keep myself flowing forwards!'

He looked back at the scientist and raised his eyebrows, but the man simply looked at him with surprise as the hands on the Doctor's golden wristwatch reached their original starting point and his time line reverted once more. He was scooted three minutes into his future, to the starting point of the loop and the apex of the pain.

One side of the Doctor's face smothered itself in grime as he collapsed prone to the sandy ground. 'The fall,' he gasped as he realised. 'Albert said he'd just seen me fall!'

Suddenly the Doctor experienced a feeling he had never felt before. His legs, chest and arms picked themselves up from the desert ground and began to soar into the air, his head and hands crooked downwards by the still-present force of gravity. 'I'm falling upwards.' He murmured to himself, the pain vanished now that the impact was yet to come. 'This is it, my one chance.'

He twisted in the air, mind racing. If he was falling he must have been pushed, and if he'd been pushed it must have been from the balcony that was rapidly drawing level with his head. He grinned to himself as he tensed his entire body. He set his jaw and growled. 'But if I don't reach the balcony,' he said, 'I can't have been pushed.'

At the last minute he kicked out his foot, hooking the toe of his boot under the textured lip of the iron floor above him, the force of his future battling the brute strength of his body. Time shuddered and ground to a halt, a movie reel with the cable unplugged. The Doctor became suspended, the nexus in a storm of conflicting pathways and alternate time lines, laughing, triumphant. 'An impossible trajectory!' he yelled, before plummeting into the past.

Chapter
15

'Sorry sir. We've brought you the, ah, Health and Safety guy.'

The Doctor cannoned onto the floor of the observation room, his guards immediately rushing to haul him up to his feet. 'I have got to stop doing this,' he croaked.

Geoff stepped forward. 'Well, well, well, what have we here?' He rubbed his palms. 'My stress reliever has arrived.'

But rather than looking scared, the Doctor merely dismissed the statement with a wave of his hand. 'Yes yes yes. Can somebody please tell me the exact time?'

Geoff stopped and stared at him.

'Sorry, sorry, introductions – I'm the Doctor, health and safety something something. And you are?'

'Colonel Geoffrey Redvers – project leader.'

The Doctor looked decidedly unimpressed. 'Good stuff. And you.' He turned his attention to the scientist. 'I've met you before although you haven't met *me* yet.'

'Dr Albert Gilroy.'

'I know, now – time anyone? Before you interrogate me? Please?' He looked around desperately. The nervous sergeant next to him checked his watch.

'Two twenty-five,' he said.

The Doctor grinned. 'Twenty minutes, good. Nothing's set in stone yet.' He looked at Albert and Geoff. 'We –' he waggled a finger between the three of them – 'have some things to sort out.'

'No,' said Geoff. '*I* have some questions to ask you.'

'Really?' said the Doctor. 'Like how I know about you transporting your androids to the courtyard as we speak, despite having never entered the compound before? Like how I know that you're about to populate the village out there,' he gestured towards the tinted window, 'with killer robots that are programmed to think they are human before you drop a nuke on them? Like how I know that there are fifty distinct models of androids, but some duplicates? Like how I know that two of them are made to act like a happily married couple called Mr and Mrs Sanderson?'

There was a shocked silence.

'Well, they're not *happily* married,' Albert interjected finally. 'That would be unrealistic. They just make do.'

Geoff set his jaw. 'How do you know all this?'

The Doctor straightened his bow tie and adopted the swagger of someone who was on top of the situation, in the hope that it would persuade the others that that was the case.

'This is going to be impossible for you to believe,' he said, 'but I am living backwards through time.'

A snort of derision echoed around the room.

'This is no laughing matter,' the Doctor scowled. 'And if you don't take me seriously you will all die.'

Geoff stopped laughing. 'Is that a threat?'

'No, it's not a threat; it's a *fact*. A series of events are about to unfold which will result in an almost one hundred per cent mortality count for you, Colonel.'

Albert was fascinated. He moved towards the prisoner and touched the sleeve of his jacket as if expecting it to explode. 'But how can you be living backwards through time?' he asked with an air of disbelief. 'You're responding to everything we say. If you know the future then you must surely know how this conversation is going to proceed. It's not possible.'

The Doctor sighed. 'Time is complicated, but its processes are based upon simple, fundamental rules – namely that the actions I perform in the future *must* have some cause in the past. But if I do something, or create a situation that is *impossible* to produce from the already determined set of events that have happened to you up until that point, then the time line shunts me into your past long enough for me to manipulate those causes so that such a situation *can* occur. If it's a small thing, then I only live forwards a few seconds, but bigger events need more interaction and so I have to reorient for longer to create the necessary chain of events.'

Albert looked around mockingly. 'But if that is the case and you *do* revert, then surely your backwards self must also be wandering around somewhere.'

'Good question!' the Doctor beamed. 'OK, I can see that what we need here are my props.' He pulled a piece of string from his pocket and laid it carefully on the map-table beside him. 'This here, is time,' he said. 'You're experiencing things from left to right: cause and effect, cause and effect. I'm experiencing things from right to left: effect, cause, effect, cause.'

He produced a pair of scissors from his pocket with a flourish. 'If I change something here,' he jabbed at a spot on the piece of string and snipped it with his scissors, 'the string to the left of this cut no longer connects because the causes don't match the effects of the right-hand section. So what happens is this – we find the beginning of the necessary causes that need to be changed on the left –' Another jab and another snip – 'and I flip this middle bit of string over, because for this section of string I am travelling forwards through time. Like I am now.' He flipped the middle section of string and began tying it back onto the end pieces.

'If I do things correctly then this right-hand knot here should be a smooth transition that now all makes cause-and-effect sense, and all you chaps will see is that I walk and talk backwards from left to right up until the first knot, then suddenly I'll start talking normally for a while whilst I alter the future until, suddenly again, I begin talking backwards once more.

'A linear progression for you, but from *my* point of view I go backwards along the string until I hit the right-hand knot, then I jump to the left-hand knot and go from forwards for this middle section, until finally I jump *back* to the left-hand knot once more to continue my backwards, right-to-left journey, thereby avoiding any overlap. Happy?'

'It's an interesting way of looking at things.' Albert scratched his stubble and thought carefully. 'But what if, during your forwards progression, the causes don't add up to the effects on the final strand?'

'Then the final strand ceases to exist altogether, a new piece of string is tied on instead and *that* becomes the new future. That's it in basic sort of terms. In reality, it's more of a ripple, running along the final piece of string and changing it into a different colour to signify a new future. Or a different texture... This analogy is confusing me now.' He grabbed the string from the table and quickly bundled it back into his pocket.

Albert sniffed and lost interest. 'OK, now I know you're insane. I just wanted to be certain. Geoff, he's yours. I'll leave you to it.' He moved towards the exit, but the Doctor grabbed him by the arm.

'What? But I thought you understood!'

'Like I said, it's a nice theory – but it's not exactly *practical*, is it? You're just showing off to try and buy some time.'

'Wait, wait. OK, fine, you got me.' The Doctor held up his hands and slipped the psychic paper out from his sleeve and into his palm. 'I'm actually from the Pentagon, access all areas, and I've been fully briefed on your mission, which is why I know everything.'

Geoff rubbed a palm over his eyes. 'This is getting silly now. First you said you were from Health and Safety, then you were travelling backwards through time, now you're a Pentagon official.'

'Ah.' The Doctor held up a finger. 'Actually I'm a Pentagon official who was working *undercover* as a Health and Safety officer. See?' he said. 'Um, just ignore the backwards-in-time bit; I knew that was never going to fly.' He thrust his pass in Geoff's face. 'Look!'

Geoff took the psychic paper gingerly and inspected it. 'Well, it appears to be genuine. Not that I believe it for one second after that little ramble.' He sighed. 'So if you *are* from the Pentagon, what are you doing here? It's not like you guys to get your hands dirty – especially with something as world-changing as this. I thought you'd all be cowering under your desks thinking up incredible alibis.'

The Doctor waggled his hands by way of explanation. 'I'm from the hands-on division.'

He paused and scratched his chin. 'But you're right, it's all a bit... extrovert this operation, isn't it? Why the nuke in the middle of the desert, and why build the town?'

'I thought you were meant to know all about this project.' Albert's eyes narrowed as he shifted his weight from foot to foot, anxious to leave.

'I *know* all about it. I just don't know *why*. That's bureaucracy for you.'

'The androids are practically indestructible,' Albert began. 'Their circuit boards and vulnerable joints are fused over once the model comes off the production line – we can't risk anybody on the other side getting hold of one. Nuking them all in one go is in fact the *cheapest* option available. And you'll notice the theme of cheapness running through this whole explanation.'

The Doctor tutted. 'Yeah, tell me about it. State-run services, always the first to cut corners. I'm always telling my Pentagon buddies we should go private; "soldiers of fortune" has a much better ring to it than "the armed forces".'

'Er, yeah. So anyway, not only are the models too expensive to maintain in the current economic climate, they're also expensive to keep still – what with the EM fields and whatnot. The village is a low-cost substitute, designed to make them think they're undercover long enough to nuke them without us blowing up a small fortune in generators at the same time. Luckily we still had a few skeleton buildings lying around from the sixties.'

The Doctor fished around in his pockets for his sonic screwdriver, but thought better of whipping it out in a room full of armed guards. 'Did you not ever consider a focused sonic pulse to dismantle the androids? I found it pretty simple myself... in theory.' He coughed quickly.

Albert looked at him like he was from another planet. 'A focused sonic what?'

The Doctor laughed bitterly. 'Oh dear. Nineteen-eighties technology against futuristic robots. You had no chance did you? Didn't you two ever stop and think that you might be getting a little ahead of yourselves?'

His tone of voice hardened. 'Didn't you two ever stop and think that maybe, just maybe, creating something where the best way to destroy it was with a *nuclear bomb* might be a bad idea? This world hangs by a thread, nations poised to destroy each other within minutes, and you know what the only thing stopping that happening is? The fact that, until now, everything the other side has produced – vehicles, soldiers, buildings – could still be destroyed with conventional weapons. It's *always* been possible to inflict casualties on your enemy without ripping apart the planet. And that fact has saved the lives of millions.' He began to pace around the room, his body tense with rage, hands gesturing wildly at the vista that lay beyond the observation glass. 'But now, but *now*… you've managed to make the impossible. A weapon that can *only* be destroyed by a nuclear weapon, where the other side has *no choice* but to use them when your androids begin carving up their people.' He stopped stone dead in his tracks. 'You know this means war?'

'It means war either way, Doctor.' Geoff's eyes were cold and unfeeling. 'That's the point. If the androids live, their existence will be discovered by the other side; if they die, we'll have broken the Test Ban Treaty, a sign of aggression against the Russians. The government want to test the limits, to escalate the situation so that the other side is forced to admit that they won't push the button, no matter what.' He paused. 'By tomorrow, we'll either have won the Cold War, or we'll all be dead. That's it – no other options.'

'Not if we can stop the nuke.'

'The plane's in the air already, there's no going back.'

'Well radio them, call it off!'

Geoff shrugged. 'I don't have the authority. It's out of my hands.'

'Well I might still have a few tricks up my sleeve regarding that anyhow.' The Doctor looked around. 'The most pressing issue at the moment is making sure your soldiers—' He broke off suddenly. 'Where's Albert?'

The scientist had vanished. Geoff snapped a gaze at the soldiers by the door.

'He just left, sir. Said he didn't have time to sit around chatting. And that's his words, not mine, sir.'

The Doctor's face went pale. 'We have to get after him. It's him I need to stop.' He rushed to the door.

'Wait, where do you think you're going?' Geoff clicked his fingers and the Doctor found himself pinned against the door by the guards. 'I'm not letting you outside, Pentagon official or not. We can't risk a rogue element in the unloading.'

'We haven't got time for this, Colonel,' the Doctor snapped. 'Albert is about to do something that will lead to the massacre of your platoon – *he's* the rogue element you should be worrying about.'

'Have we switched back to your "I've seen the future" story now, then?'

The Doctor yanked his hands free. 'Go with whatever story you like, but I have to go. Five minutes with Albert, that's all I need, then you can load me on a truck to the village and I'll be out of sight and mind.'

Geoff faltered at the sincerity in the stranger's voice. 'Albert wouldn't betray me.'

'He doesn't *know* he's going to betray you!'

'What's he going to do?'

The Doctor turned and looked Geoff in the eye before muttering one single, heartbreaking word. 'Isley.'

Geoff let out a yell, his suspicions confirmed. 'I knew it. I knew he couldn't keep his distance – the extra programs he wrote for her were nonsense. I told him time and time again he was putting us all at risk with that music player business.'

The Doctor raised his eyebrows.

'Five minutes, Doctor, then I'm putting you on the trucks.'

But the Doctor was already out of the door, boots clattering down the iron staircase. 'Thank you!'

Albert tapped a nearby captain softly on the shoulder. 'I'll take it from here,' he whispered, as the last of the androids were unloaded from the truck. He had already retrieved his bag from the front cabin and was toying nervously with the Walkman in his hand. He wrapped the headphone wire around a finger, then unwrapped it again as the captain turned his face to acknowledge him.

'Don't do this, Albert.' The voice was low and quiet, but its authority was undeniable.

Albert turned, quickly stuffing the Walkman into his coat pocket. 'What are you doing here? Shouldn't you be cuffed to a radiator or something by now?'

The Doctor pushed through the row of soldiers that divided the two men until he was face to face with the scientist. 'You don't understand what you are about to do.'

'I'm just...' Albert's eyes filled with tears. 'I just want to say goodbye. What's wrong with that?'

'She's a machine, Albert, she doesn't understand the way you see her. She's not even aware of how you feel. How could she be?'

Albert choked, as the Doctor gently took his hand and began leading the man away from the lorry. The scientist protested and tried to pull away but the Doctor's grip was firm and unyielding. He nodded to the captain to resume the unloading.

'I know what it's like, Albert, to love something that you created, but it's not *real* love, is it? It's pride – you just think you're in love because you made her look so beautiful.'

'She is beautiful.'

'They all are, Albert, everything you've created is incredible. You're decades ahead of your time, you know that? But they're not people, they're weapons. You can't forget that – they're guns dressed up like men and women.'

As the Doctor backed away, Albert following reluctantly, he waved a hand behind his back to a group of soldiers who had just finished playing cards around a small circle of barrels in the shade of the officer's mess. They vacated their seats without a word.

'I've never been in love, Doctor.' Albert slumped onto the cool steel seat.

The Doctor settled beside him and rested his head against the corrugated iron wall. 'It's never too late.'

Albert laughed. 'Of course it is. This was my life. *She* was my life. There is nothing for me beyond this.' He turned, suddenly intense. 'Have you really seen the future?'

The Doctor opened his eyes and tilted his head. 'Yes,' he said with complete sincerity. 'You told me what happened when I found you amongst the survivors. You said that you'd walked Isley to the dead zone and someone shouted something. It triggered the military programming – no one had a chance. Geoff had no choice but to put you on a truck. You died in the village at Isley's hand.'

His honesty was brutal, and it hit Albert like a bullet through the heart.

'But the point is,' the Doctor continued, 'you wouldn't have done it if you'd known what would happen. It might seem like the most important thing in the universe to say goodbye to her now, but it won't be worth what happens next – you said so yourself. You *told me* yourself.'

Albert leaned forward and rested his head in his hands. He took a deep breath, a long sniff, and when he looked back at the Doctor his eyes were dead and cold. 'You're right.'

The Doctor smiled weakly. 'I'm always right,' he said.

'So what happens now?'

'Nothing and everything.' The Doctor shrugged. 'The future is already changed – you didn't trigger the massacre. That was it. We changed history by having a conversation.'

'But... everything you lived through...?'

'Will soon have no longer existed,' he finished Albert's sentence for him. 'Time will ripple forwards from this point, and in this version all these soldiers will live. You'll never see what I have seen.'

Albert smiled faintly through the tears, his cheeks glistening in the shadow. 'Then shouldn't we be looking a bit happier?'

The Doctor turned away. 'You should,' he said.

'What's wrong?' Albert was concerned once more.

'It's the bomb, the bomb you dropped – or will drop in an hour's time. That's why I'm stuck living backwards, I managed to halt it at the point of detonation but to extinguish the explosion completely I was forced to dissipate the energy into the past.' He leant forward now. 'But don't you see? I've changed things, changed the future – including the hour that leads up to the bomb being dropped. It's a new piece of string; the old time line won't exist any more.'

'So all that energy dissipation...'

'Will be lost. The lost energy will coalesce at the point of impact and explode into the future once again. I can't stop the bomb going off, your government is still going to ignite a war and worst of all, and *worst* of all...' The Doctor struggled to sustain his composure. 'My friends were in Appletown, at the instant of detonation. I've condemned them to death to save your men.'

Albert looked aghast. 'Is there nothing you can do?'

The Doctor looked at his watch. 'Not until I revert to my backwards state. I have to finish the loop with you and Geoff loading me into the truck – if I try and preserve as much of the old time line as possible, it might take longer for the energy to reach the critical point. Once this forward loop finishes, I'll be travelling through my arrival at the base, reversed from your point of view.'

'On the bicycle?'

The Doctor rubbed his chin. 'Now there's a good idea.'

'But how does this reversed state end? Are you stuck like this for ever?'

'I hope not. The plan was to travel backwards until the explosion was completely dissipated, then, fingers crossed, I'd snap back to the instant the reversion began, pick up my companions and tell the Colonel to drop a second bomb the moment they were safe.'

Albert chuckled incredulously. 'A *second* bomb? Do you think we're made of money?'

The Doctor's glance made him stop short. 'I don't care about money; I care about Amy and Rory. Their lives are beyond value.' He ruffled a hand through his hair. 'Anyway, it's irrelevant now.'

Albert got slowly to his feet. 'Well, go and warn them now! Tell them to stay away from the village!'

'We haven't arrived yet.' The Doctor shrugged. 'And every minute this backwards loop continues takes me further away from that moment.' He leant forward and stood up to join the scientist, moving past him in the direction of the covered walkway that led to the courtyard. His shoulders were hunched, his head hung low, the gait of a defeated man. Albert had to jog to catch up with him, drawing alongside as the Doctor strode beneath the first strips of artificial light.

'You know what?' Albert said with a voice made of steel. 'I don't think you do care about your friends very much.'

The Doctor rounded on him, and the scientist started at the sight of the stranger's face – a tight mask of rage and grief. 'How dare you,' the Doctor hissed. 'You have no idea.'

Undaunted, Albert continued. 'Look at you, Doctor – a man of impossible things. You claim to be able to diffuse the effects of a nuclear bomb, you live backwards through time, you've saved my life and the lives of everyone on this base with nothing but a piece of string...' He dropped his hands to his sides in exasperation. 'Does that sound like the behaviour of a man who just... gives up?'

The Doctor looked at him silently for a full minute, then embraced him. 'You're right,' he said quietly. 'Thank you.'

They walked the last few metres in silence, a pair of guards solemnly pulling open the great iron doors to the courtyard as they stepped, blinking,

into the natural light once more. The citizens
had been almost completely transferred to the
waiting vehicles at the exit to the compound and
the Doctor solemnly took his place at the head of
the final queue, boots crunching on the sand as he
turned to face the scientist, his back to the trucks.
He looked around and snapped his fingers.

'Guards! If you would please escort me to one
of the trucks. Backwards, if you don't mind.'

He checked his watch. 'In thirty seconds,' he
added.

The five soldiers began to gather hesitantly
around the incongruous figure, faces tilted to
the balcony above in search of confirmation.
Albert followed their gaze and saw Geoff, leaning
nonchalantly over the iron railings. He nodded
solemnly and scratched his face, still unsure why
he was permitting this.

Albert gave a knowing nod to the Doctor, who
smiled and returned the motion. 'I will not be
beaten,' he said, and took a step backwards.

Albert didn't notice the switch, the subliminal
flash and hiccup in time as the man he had been
talking to only seconds before was catapulted
backwards half an hour. But the look of
unfamiliarity in the prisoner's eyes as he was led
away and the unnatural assuredness with which
he took each step backwards, told him everything

he needed to know.

He turned away quietly and spotted the nervous sergeant as he prepared to board up the rear of the first truck. He jogged over to him with a swift 'Hey'.

The sergeant nodded, and then looked up in surprise as he found Albert's Walkman shoved quickly into his hands. 'Sir?' he enquired.

'Can you give this to Isley?' Albert asked as he unravelled the headphones from his pocket and coiled it up in the man's palm. 'She's in the truck at the back.'

'Uh, yeah, sure. Anything you say, sir.'

'It'll make the journey go quicker if she's got music to listen to,' Albert explained. 'And if there's any tape left when she's unloaded, it'll act as an extra reinforcement to her reset and keep you guys safe a bit longer.'

'Oh right. Well, thanks, Dr Gilroy.' The sergeant coiled the wire tightly around the player. 'I'll do that.'

Albert's relief was plain to see and he opened his arms to give the soldier a brief hug of thanks, but he thought better of it upon seeing the soldier's frightened face and instead stuffed his hands into his pockets awkwardly. 'Take care of her,' he said finally. 'She's not like the others. She's special, you know?'

'If you say so, sir.' The sergeant raised his hand in a half salute, but the scientist was already hurrying away.

Chapter
16

Colorado, 28 August 1981, 6.07 p.m.

The smoke was warm and thick as it coiled around the pair, huddled in the corner of the upstairs bedroom. Amy's head rested gently on her fiancé's lap as the thick cloud filled her lungs and lulled her to sleep. Rory too was struggling to stay awake; he ran his fingers idly through the girl's soft red hair, the pain in his arm reduced to a dull, soothing throb.

There was something he should be doing.

'Escape!' The word was muffled inside his head, and Rory was unsure whether he had actually spoken it out loud. But the urge remained nonetheless.

He peered into the blackening haze and, in the soft glow from the window, he managed to discern the faint outline of the doorframe above the stack of furniture which seemed to have fallen in the way. It took a few seconds for Rory to remember that it was he who had put them there. 'Well, it seemed like a good idea at the time,' he told himself.

Carefully, he rolled Amy from his lap and gently onto the floor, twitching his foot to relieve the cramp. She stirred quietly, and Rory tilted his head to one side and smiled affectionately, then stopped himself. 'What am I doing?' he muttered. A sharp slap to the face and Amy was awake, yelping in pain.

'Ow! What did you do that for?' she scowled, rubbing her cheek.

'Because we were about to suffocate to death, that's what,' Rory called over his shoulder as he flung himself prostrate on the wooden floorboards. 'Now stay low, the smoke'll be thinnest near the floor.'

'*More* crawling? I am so sick of crawling.' Amy lifted herself groggily to her hands and knees and began to follow him. 'Ouch!' she declared. 'The floor's burning!'

'That's because it *is* burning.'

'All right, good point.'

Rory reached the edge of the wardrobe and snatched at it with a hand, hauling himself up and into the thicker strata of smoke that was gently descending to the floor. He yelled with pain as the injury in his arm stabbed at his muscle. Amy took a deep breath and joined him, yanking at the desk until it nearly slid over on top of her. She jumped to the side just in time and the drawers smashed a hole in the weakened floorboards by her feet. A sinister orange glow blossomed into the air around them as the flames in the kitchen below lit up the clouds.

'Yeah, I think we're running out of time,' Rory stated matter-of-factly. He held his breath and heaved at the wardrobe, inching it away from the door. It squealed along the floorboards and they bowed with the weight.

'The floor's not going to hold.' Amy was already at the door, pulling it open as far as it would go. Just a little further and she'd be able to squeeze through. The bowing frame creaked loudly one final time, and suddenly Amy was on the other side, her eyes watering as the smoke on the landing smothered her face.

'Push from the other side!' Rory shouted.

With a concerted effort, the wardrobe slid a few more centimetres. Then the floor gave way completely.

'Rory!' Amy yelled a warning as the blackened wood crumbled and splintered away. Her fiancé dived for the handle, catching it just in time to avoid the flames below and swinging his other hand up to grab Amy's as his sweaty palms slipped on the roasting metal.

They tumbled onto the landing, coughing and staggering over to the edge of the thin corridor where the structure was still sound.

'Where now?' Amy spluttered as the smoke filled her lungs.

Nursing his burnt hand, Rory edged his way to the top of the staircase and shied away at the heat. Huge flames licked their way up the banisters and the stairs were all but disintegrated.

'OK, we're going to have to jump for it.' He gestured through one of the doors on the opposite side of the landing. 'I just hope this couple built a compost heap in their back garden.'

'Made out of what? They don't eat!' Amy was at his side as they pushed into a rear bedroom, still relatively untouched by the flames.

'Hush, you'll jinx it.' Rory held up a palm. He squinted his eyes and shuffled cautiously to the window as if not being able to see would magically make his hopes come true. But when he opened them and stared down onto the terraced back garden, his expression changed to that of sheer incredulity. 'Well,' he said after a long pause, 'I really wasn't expecting *that*!'

'Is it safe?' Amy hung back.

'Uh, yeah.' Rory was still speechless.

She pressed her face against the glass to see what he was staring at, and then she too opened her mouth in surprise.

'Whoa,' she said faintly.

Displayed before them, and mown into the lawn with a large, looping script across the back garden of the opposite house, were the words *Follow me*, and then what Amy could swear was a smiley face. Both the letters and the face were upside down. She traced the line of the message with her finger as it trailed off to one side and she saw that the author had scrawled a rambling path through hedges and shattered fences that spanned the length of the terrace. She tried to trace it to its end, but the rest of the trail became obscured in the shadow of a series of larger buildings several houses down, and she lost it in the darkness.

'Do you think it's...?' Rory trailed off.

'Well, of course it's the Doctor.' A slow smile was spreading across Amy's face. 'I told you he wouldn't leave us!'

'Not quite the TARDIS materialising in the nick of time though, is it?'

Amy tutted. 'There's having your cake and

there's eating it, Rory. Think of it this way – you get to spend more time alone with me.' She winked.

'That means you want me to go down first and catch you, doesn't it?'

Amy slid the window smoothly open and flourished her hand. 'My, what a sweet offer, you are quite the gentleman!'

Rory hit the ground and rolled in a way that would have made his primary-school gym instructor proud, but it still hurt. He scanned his surroundings quickly, but there was no sign of any hostile movement in the gently swaying bushes that hissed and popped at the small drizzle of burning ash and embers as they floated gently across the gardens.

'Clear!' Rory hissed up at the open window before his face was swiftly covered by Amy's jacket. He pulled it out of his eyes, just in time to catch his fiancée as she dropped into his arms with a small squeak.

She turned her face to look at him, their noses brushing. 'Are you going to carry me the rest of the way then, lover-boy?'

Rory plonked her on the turf. 'Not likely.'

Amy rubbed her bruised rear. 'I knew this chivalry wouldn't last for ever. Come on, then!' An instant later and she was pushing through the battered remnants of the privet hedges towards the opposite garden.

'No sign of pursuit.' Rory glanced over his shoulder. 'If they thought there was no way we were going to escape, I feel quite hurt. We don't look *that* inept, do we?'

'Hush, you'll jinx it,' Amy replied. 'Now's the time to act, not look for motivation.'

The late afternoon air was cooler now that the pair had moved away from the warmth of the burning building and the sun cast a long shadow over them as they stopped short in the middle of the turf, the message splayed out around them.

'How did he know what was going to happen to us?' Rory asked quietly. 'He always seems to know.'

Amy looked up cautiously at the dark outline of the house in front of her, tinged with an orange glow from the flames behind. 'I don't think he did. Otherwise he'd have written it the right way up.' She pondered for a moment. 'No, he must have assumed we would go to this house.' She pointed at the building in front of her.

'But why?'

'Let's find out.' She flashed Rory a swift grin and was already pushing open the sliding patio doors before he could protest.

The young man was left pointing a limp finger

in the direction of the demolished fences, his other hand stuffed in his pocket. 'Can't we just, you know, do what the message says?' He tailed off and sighed in exasperation. 'Fine, I'm coming!'

The house was dark and dusty and smelt of sawdust; Rory was sick of the smell of sawdust. He found Amy flat on her stomach and worming her way towards the front entrance. His shoes thudded softly as he approached the prone figure and she waved him down without looking.

'Quiet!' she hissed. 'I'm going to open the front door.'

Rory looked around quickly, and spotted what Amy must have noticed an instant beforehand. Faint footprints ran across the entrance hall, softly outlined in the dust, and his eyes followed them as they made a beeline for the stairs. There were two sets of prints – a pair of trainers and a pair of heeled boots and Rory's heart sank as he realised where they were.

The front door squeaked ever so slightly as it opened but there was no sign of movement above the garden gate that Rory could see through the gap. Neither he nor Amy were surprised to see the broken bits of timber frame and glass that littered the lawn in front of them. But there was something missing.

'Where's Albert's body?' Amy asked as she

quickly pushed the door back onto the latch.

'I dunno. Taken as a trophy?' Rory shrugged.

'They're robots, not tribesmen.'

'Probably best to worry about that once we've found the Doctor, eh?'

'I suppose.' Amy sidled back through the hallway towards the rear doors once more.

Rory stopped and waited for a few seconds, ears searching for any sign of pursuit or discovery, but there was no noise apart from the gentle tapping of Amy's heels. He turned and followed her into the back garden.

As the patio doors slid shut, the house became still once more, a deep, graveside silence. Then a dark silhouette stirred into action from its vantage point in the shadows at the top of the stairs.

'They've been trimming the hedge-edges!' Rory muttered as he dodged and weaved through the trampled flowerbeds and broken fences that marked the winding path through the rear gardens.

'The whats?'

'The. Hedge. Edges,' Rory repeated slowly.

Amy grinned. 'Just one more time.'

'The hedgedgedges. Happy now?'

'Very.' She smiled sweetly.

'Look.' He reached out a hand and brushed

it along the rounded curves of a broken garden border, then gestured to the clippings on the ground. 'It's like they didn't realise the path wasn't meant to be here, and they just incorporated it into their gardening.'

'But that would mean that this path must have been made before they arrived.'

Rory pondered. 'And definitely before *we* arrived. What on earth is the Doctor doing?'

'Ours not to reason why…' Amy recited. 'Ours just to stay alive.'

They had crossed nearly a dozen gardens by now and Amy could see the end in sight: a large warehouse at the end of the block with a hole smashed into the side the size of a small car. 'Sheesh,' she muttered. 'He's had a bit of fun making this, hasn't he? How come we're never around to join in when he starts smashing things up?'

'We just demolished a house!' Rory pointed to the plume of smoke still billowing out from the broken skeleton of the house behind them. 'I'm trying my best!'

'And you're very good at it.' Amy placed a reassuring hand on his shoulder as they drew closer to the warehouse. 'But it's all been a bit too easy, hasn't it? I mean, why didn't the androids surround the building we were in, or acknowledge the path in their lawns and do something about it?'

'Like I said, maybe they just assumed it was a part of the landscape. Or...' He paused. 'They could all be inside the warehouse, waiting to ambush us.'

More cautiously now, they approached either side of the gaping hole and peered tentatively into the deep gloom inside, contrasted further by the brightness of the afternoon sun. The highlights of a fairly large metal object were all that they could pick out, and Rory edged silently inside.

He blinked, waiting for his eyes to adjust until eventually the pitch black shadows mellowed into grey shapes and he realised that the object was a large, petrol-driven, ride-on lawnmower, parked in the centre of the space. The tracks they had followed clearly ended beneath its chunky tyres. But it wasn't the machine that Rory had fixed his frightened gaze on; it was the person slumped casually on the modest seat, arms resting gently in her lap.

It was Isley.

Chapter

17

Colorado, 28 August 1981, 6.30 p.m.

The android's eyes flickered around the shadows of the warehouse, amplifying the light and searching for signs of movement. She had been waiting for five minutes and twenty-seven seconds when the whitened greys of the space caught a movement behind one of the tall wooden supports. Her head swivelled to focus.

A girl – brown eyes, red hair, pale skin – was moving quietly and swiftly across the side of one wall. Isley flexed her joints in preparation for the kill, a cat, coiled and ready to spring. It took a fraction of a second for her to leap to her feet and lunge towards the target.

Suddenly she was jerked backwards, the wire that still connected the headphone speakers that bounced lazily over her shoulders tightening around her neck. With her head racing through analyses of possible attack patterns and counter moves the girl might exhibit, she hadn't noticed the second target.

A click, a snap, a spin, a second click and the sound of a button being depressed registered in her brain. The cassette hissed through the blank opening of the tape for three seconds before the music began, softly drifting into her sensory circuits from the speakers around her neck.

Rory swore. 'Where's the volume slidey thing? Oh wait, no, here it is.'

The music increased in pitch and Isley's head slumped forward onto her chest.

'Cut that a bit fine.' Amy moved over swiftly, trying to avoid the glazed eyes of the android.

'I was the one whose neck was in reach!' Rory reminded her as he waved a hand across Isley's face. 'It looks like the magic music works then.'

'Can we talk to her?'

'Albert said she wouldn't respond to anyone except people he'd instructed her to communicate with.'

'But he *did* instruct her to communicate with

us. Didn't he?'

As if a switch had suddenly been flipped in her head, Isley swivelled to face Rory. The pair started, but she made no further motion. Eventually her lips parted and she spoke, a flat, emotionless monotone.

'Where's Albert?'

Amy and Rory glanced at each other.

'See?' Amy said.

'Albert has not instructed me to communicate with you.' Isley clarified, 'But I am not restricted by my original programming.' There was a pause. 'Where is Albert?' she reiterated.

Rory clasped his hands together and leaned forward angrily. 'You killed him, don't you remember that? You threw him out of a window. We were there, we saw it.'

Isley shook her head. 'No.'

'No? What do you mean "no"?'

'That isn't what happened.'

Amy crouched in front of the young woman. 'Then what *did* happen, Isley?' she asked carefully.

'You and you,' she looked from Amy to Rory, 'discovered me in my room in the house. It took three minutes, forty-two seconds for my system to reboot effectively after the military programmes activated, a process delayed due to the length of time I was shut down by the electromagnetic field. By the time I was active, you had already left the building.'

'But Albert was there. You threw him from the upstairs window – the wreckage is all over the front lawn!'

Again Isley shook her head, almost in time to the music. 'I jumped through the window myself in pursuit. Albert never entered the village.'

Rory was thoroughly confused by now. 'A lying robot. Now I've seen everything!' he declared loudly, waving his hands in exasperation.

Amy held up a placating finger. 'Hold on a second,' she said before resuming her line of questioning. 'Isley, when was the last time you saw Albert?'

'The military compound, in the dead zone between transports, he was talking to your...' Her eye ticked as she searched her dictionary. 'Friend?' she suggested eventually.

'The Doctor!' Rory pinched his nose with a finger and thumb and squinted as he tried to get his head around what he was hearing.

'He's changed the past,' Amy whispered.

'Or he will change the past.'

'Were *we* at the compound, Isley?'

'No.'

Amy looked to Rory. 'Well either he's changed

the past whilst we're here or we're going to die before he comes to pick us up.'

'That's a comforting thought. Thanks, Amy. But how can he have changed the past without us noticing?' Rory was getting frustrated. 'We remember what happened!'

'Yeah, but we're time travellers! We're not even meant to exist in this time and place. If messing about with time is going to change our memories, where would you stop?'

Rory circled the lawnmower, his mind racing. 'That still doesn't explain why the Doctor's popped off to do that and left us here with nothing but a lawnmower message for help.'

'He saved Albert. I think that's reason enough,' Amy snapped.

'As far as I can see this whole thing is because of Albert anyway.'

Amy sighed and turned away, refocusing her attention on the android. 'Were you waiting for us here? Why?'

'I can read. Basic tracking programs are improved and refined by application; defenceless targets are useful for practice. It was logical that you would obey the instruction described by this machine.'

'Can't any of the other models read?' Amy raised an eyebrow.

It was with an almost mocking tone that Isley responded. 'No. I have been operational for exactly five years. My data assimilation, learning capabilities and military programming are, on average, tenfold superior to the other models – most of which have not yet applied their basic military tactics.'

Rory snorted. 'So they might be indestructible killing machines, but they're stupid indestructible killing machines.'

'Except for me,' Isley interjected.

Rory was surprised that the android had responded and was unsure whether she was merely stating the facts or whether she actually sounded smug. 'Yes, except for you,' he finally agreed. He turned to his fiancé. 'Right, what are we supposed to do with her now? We might have an hour's grace, but she's still lethal.'

Amy shrugged. 'Like you said, she's indestructible. I suggest we find out what the Doctor wants us to do in here, then put a safe distance between us and the end of that tape as quickly as possible.'

There was silence for a few minutes except for the quiet guitar riff coming from the speakers around the robot's neck, its sound dampened by the dust that coated the floor. The pair looked around.

'Well I've got—'

'No idea.' Amy finished. 'Me neither.'

Rory ran a hand through his hair. 'Isley? You seem in a helpful mood. Any ideas?'

Isley twitched. 'Where's Albert?' she said simply.

'I don't know, lady; probably where you last saw him!' Exasperated, Rory ran over to the mower, now highlighted in a pool of golden light, its green paint coloured a dull orange. 'No note, Doctor? Come on! Give us something!'

'There!' Amy ran over to the huge wooden doors of warehouse, where a tiny post-it had been slapped on the wooden bolt that ran across the entrance. She peeled it off and examined it, squinting through the yellow haze.

'Well? What does it say?' Rory demanded.

'It doesn't make any sense.'

'He *never* makes any sense!' Rory called back. 'Just read it anyway!'

'Uh, OK.' She cleared her throat and began. '"You have exactly nine minutes and twenty-four seconds to get to the town square—"'

Rory looked incredulous. 'How on earth could he know exactly what time we'd pick up that note? It's tiny for a start!'

'I've not finished.' Amy ran her finger across the looping script. 'What it *says* is, "You have exactly nine minutes and twenty-four seconds to get to the town square *from the moment the buildings begin to disintegrate*." There, see? Not so magic.'

But Rory wasn't listening. 'Amy.' His voice began to shake. 'How did you manage to read a post-it note in a room that was pitch black when we entered?' He held out his hand, puncturing a column of deep golden light that was flooding downwards from above. 'And why has everything got so... *orange* all of a sudden?'

Amy's eyes widened as, suddenly, a bright shaft of daylight flooded into the centre of the warehouse, picking Rory out in pure white highlights. Her hair ruffled and tugged at her scalp and she could feel a wind whipping up around her. Both of them looked up at the same moment, eyes moving slowly, dreading what they were about to see.

The roof of the warehouse was coming apart, planks and tiles flaking and shattering as they were picked up and scattered by the wind. Through the gaping holes they could see the sky, but now it had been transformed to a sickly yellow and grotesquely deformed clouds scudded over their heads, warping and stretching as they watched.

Rory extended his arms, palms uplifted as if presenting the sky to those around him. 'Ruddy hell,' he shouted over the gale. 'It's the end of the world!'

There was a kick, a growl and the lawnmower motor spluttered into life. Rory turned to find Amy astride the metal seat, beckoning to him to hop on behind her. He had to read her lips to work out what she was shouting.

'I think our nine minutes and twenty-four seconds might have already started!' she yelled.

Rory leapfrogged over the rear engine, slamming his hip-bone against an awkwardly placed piece of metal. Amy took his roar of pain as a sign to get the hell out of there, and she slammed her foot down hard on the accelerator. Rory wrapped his arms around his fiancée's waist as the beast began to rumble towards the bolted exit, steadily gathering speed.

'Wait!'

Rory turned his head in surprise. Isley was jogging alongside, the faint vocals of the music in the headphones bouncing around her neck barely audible over the bass of the wind and her sandy hair was tinged almost blood-red in the apocalyptic light.

'Wait!' she repeated. 'Where's Albert?'

But they didn't have time to wait. Rory turned back to see the gates looming perilously close. 'Shouldn't we have opened them first?'

Amy smiled to herself. 'Why should the Doctor

get to have all the fun?' she replied, thumbing a button on the dashboard. The lawnmower blades unfolded from the sides of the vehicle, spinning wildly as they approached the exit and Amy felt Rory's arms squeeze tight around her as both of them dipped their faces into their chests in preparation for the impact.

There was a brutal, crunching sound, like that of an enormous buzz-saw, and the couple were showered with splinters and sawdust as, with a hefty crack, the gates split, and the momentum of the vehicle carried them out onto the open road.

'Wahoo!' Amy yelled in triumph and held her palm up for Rory to high-five. He did so with a loud wolf whistle and leant over Amy's shoulder to kiss her sawdust-coated cheek.

'I've got to hand it to the Doctor,' he shouted in her ear. 'He certainly knows how to liven things up!'

Chapter

18

Colorado, 28 August 1981, 2.04 p.m.

'Well, I've got to hand it to myself: I certainly know how to liven things up.' The Doctor wiped down his sonic screwdriver with a rag from his pocket and slipped it into the inside of his jacket before wiping down the side of the lawnmower once more. 'There you go, all nice and turbo-charged. I'll put it on your tab shall I, Amy, Rory?' He looked around sadly, before his confidence got the better of him. 'I always waste my best lines when I'm alone,' he sighed.

The light from outside cast a slanted beam through the smashed-up hole in the back wall that almost touched his boots and he crouched down to write a post-it in the glow.

A moment later and he'd stuck the sticker across the barred front entrance to the warehouse and was ducking outside once more, taking a moment to admire the last ten minutes' handiwork, his hands on his hips and a wry smile across his face. 'Let's just hope the androids don't notice anything out of the ordinary when they arrive,' he muttered, mopping his brow and unwittingly leaving a streak of oil across his forehead.

He pulled his bike away from where it had been resting against a nearby wall and began to pedal out into the road and towards the centre of Appletown. 'And they said it was impossible to pedal a bike backwards,' he said to himself with a grin.

A few minutes later, the familiar blue shape of the TARDIS came into view around a corner. The Doctor greeted it with a wave and a whoop.

'Hello, beautiful!' he shouted.

His back wheel skidded round as he applied the brakes, and he looked up at the white-rimmed windows as he dismounted. 'What? Giving me the silent treatment, are you? Well, I don't blame you, to be honest. I've been an ungrateful Doctor, that's for sure. You go to all this trouble to save our lives, and I go and mess it up at the last minute – for another bunch of idiot humans, no less.' He reached out a hand to stroke the painted wooden frame. 'You know, one day I'll find a less self-destructive species to hang around with, and you and I can live a much quieter life... Ouch!' he yelped. 'You're hotting up pretty bad in there. Can't be much longer till the bomb's back to its full potential.' He pointed accusingly. 'If you didn't talk so much...'

In a flurry of movement he pulled off his jacket, wrapping it around his arm again to open the door. Taking a deep breath, he stepped over the threshold, threw his jacket onto the hat stand inside and slammed the door shut behind him.

All was quiet for a few minutes until suddenly he popped his head out into the sunlight once more. Cautiously he looked both ways then reached out to grab the bike by its handles.

'Yoink!' he declared. 'Happy Christmas, me!' before wheeling it inside and shutting the doors behind him.

In the vast interior of the TARDIS, a war was being waged and the air conditioning seemed to be on the verge of losing as the Doctor bounded up the steps to the console, snapping his braces tight against his shoulders. Above his head, the flaming ball of the nuclear bomb rippled and flashed in its stasis field.

The Doctor jabbed an angry finger at it. 'You – keep cooking away all you like, I'll be rid of you in a moment, and you –' He turned his attention to the console – 'You and I have some things to do. Three things, in fact…' He held up three fingers, then stopped and lowered his hand thoughtfully. Somehow this just didn't seem quite dramatic enough. 'Wait there!' he called over his shoulder before disappearing down a branching corridor.

The Doctor returned seconds later carrying a flip chart and set it up in front of the monitor. 'Right!' He tore off the first page and let it tumble to the floor before scribbling furiously with a marker pen. 'Three things! First – we need to rescue Amy and Rory.' He flipped the pen at the scanner. 'And I've already started to sort that, so you'd better make my post-it note come true. Second – we need to eject the bomb and use it to destroy Appletown and its entire population of sinister robots. Third… OK, I'm going to be honest with you here, this one's the toughie. Third,' he repeated, 'we need to eject the bomb and let it detonate *without* producing a mushroom cloud. If the Russians spot the test, I refuse to bear witness to the beginning of a war. I'm sure Albert or Geoff will be clever enough to come up with a cover story for all the radiation and stuff.' He stopped and paused. 'Lord knows they owe me that.'

He underlined the three points clearly, then again for emphasis, before finally making a dash for the console. 'We can have it all today!' he shouted with a roar of determination. 'I promise you, today we are going to have it all!'

The control panel sparked and flashed like a Catherine wheel as he jumped from lever to lever, oblivious to the burns on his hands as he prepared the TARDIS to jump back to the moment of impact. The scanner flashed and clicked on, displaying a fuzzy grey meter at almost ninety-seven per cent and the clock beneath continued to tick through negative time as the craft neared the end of its loop.

'OK, I'm taking the safeties off!' the Doctor shouted, just in case the console hadn't had time to catch up with his flurry of inputs. 'When we snap back to the point of capture, I want you to jettison the cargo and continue on – overshoot the target by... I dunno...' He looked at his watch. 'An hour and thirty-seven minutes? That should spread the impact thinly enough.'

The size of the time difference dawned on the Doctor. 'Oh Amy, Rory, over an hour and a half at the mercy of those monsters?' He crossed his fingers. 'I bet you gave 'em hell!'

Suddenly, the stasis field behind him jerked outwards in all directions as the bomb's energy returned to full capacity, and the Doctor was hurled across the control room, hitting the curved side of the wall and sliding down into the shadowy space beneath the gantry.

'This is it!' he shouted. 'Break the loop!'

The TARDIS juddered and shook as it flipped and reoriented around its own time line before rocketing into the future, groaning and screeching as it tore into the reconfigured chain of events that the Doctor had crafted. The Doctor staggered to his feet; across the room he could see the main view screen, local time strobing across it in loud bursts of light.

2.37, 2.52, 3.10, 3.40, 4.03…

Mustering all his strength, he hauled himself over the edge of the parapet and his hands burned as he crawled over to the console and grabbed the handbrake for support. He lifted his chest to prop himself against the control panel as his right hand felt for the correct lever.

4.15, 4.27, 4.40, 4.51, 4.57, 5.01…

'Detonation point! Eject and overshoot!' The Doctor nearly pulled the lever off in his hand, and above him the stasis field glowed white, swelling in a nanosecond before snapping out of the TARDIS's interior dimensions with a sonic boom of repressurising air that made the Doctor reel with sudden deafness.

5.15, 5.26, 5.55, 6.10, 6.23, 6.45…

The Doctor slumped over the handbrake and, with his last ounce of strength, depressed the button and forced it on. He collapsed to the floor with exhaustion, watching the glow of the central column grind and slow as the TARDIS jumped and skidded through time before coming to a halt in the middle of Appletown village square at 6.49 p.m. on 28 August 1981.

'They're coming for us!' Rory turned his head as far as he dared. He was sure a ride-on lawnmower shouldn't be travelling this fast.

'Let 'em.' Amy grinned. 'They might be indestructible but they'll stay away from these blades if they're clever.'

All around them, the citizens of Appletown were tearing down front doors, vaulting over garden hedges and sprinting out into the road in pursuit. The steady crowd was growing stronger with every passing second, each model travelling at top speed, their strides pounding the ground in unison.

All around the couple, the wooden-clad buildings were crumbling and disintegrating, tiles and timbers cast into the air as they dissolved in the fire like sugar in tea. The sky was filled with angry clouds – low, amber monsters that blotted out the sun and transformed the afternoon into an eerie twilight.

'You know we thought we were going to be nuked?' Amy called over her shoulder as she swerved to avoid the owner of the coffee shop who had thrown himself onto the street from a top-floor window.

Rory was too busy holding on for dear life to care at this point. 'Oh yeah?'

'Well, I think it just happened.'

The ground was on fire now, the stones melting beneath the thundering wheels of the mower. A pack of androids rounded an upcoming corner, and Rory retched as he saw the melted, stringy plastic that dripped and fell from their faces. They stumbled to their knees as the mower tore past, metal sparking and shattering as they disintegrated.

'I suppose there's no point asking why we're not affected?'

Amy shook her head. 'I don't know the answers, but I know someone who owes us some!'

She pointed ahead of them.

'Oh, mama, I never thought I'd see that again!' cried Rory.

The dark shape of the TARDIS was grinding into existence at the end of the road. Dust and debris tore across its faded outline as the howling roar of the engines threatened to take on the wind itself.

There was a sharp thud and the mower skidded sideways, Amy wrestling for control as a wheel and both of the machine's blades snapped away from the chassis. 'The mower's gone squiffy!' she shouted through gritted teeth.

'It's in the middle of a *nuclear explosion*!' Rory exclaimed. 'Just keep it straight, we've got enough momentum to slide the last bit.'

The metal crumbled away from their legs, red-hot dust spraying across their shins as they skidded across the desert sand, Rory's trainers curling and smoking as they hit the ground.

'Doctor!' Amy shouted as they prepared themselves for impact with the TARDIS. 'Open the doors!'

As if viewed through a dream, a bright haze flooded out onto the path ahead as the double doors of the TARDIS were flung open to receive its guests. A silhouette slouched against the frame and, with the flourish of a circus ringmaster, the Doctor beckoned the pair into its vast interior, just as the mower exploded into a cloud of liquid metal behind them. Casually, the Doctor reached out a hand and caught a small black box before tossing the object into the air and slipping it into his pocket.

He tugged his forelock at what was left of Appletown and – with a cheery 'Goodbye for ever!' – he slammed the doors behind him as the storm exploded outside.

A second later and the TARDIS had faded away.

'Aaaand bingo!' With a sweep of his wrist, the Doctor crossed out the first item on his flip chart and stood back to see all three of his goals thoroughly scribbled out. He rubbed his chin. 'Should have put "Save Rory and Amy" at the bottom – would have made it much more satisfying to work through that way.' He looked at the bedraggled pair in the corner of the room. 'But between you and me *they* –' He nodded his head conspiratorially – 'probably wouldn't have appreciated that.'

He was interrupted by a loud flapping sound as Rory tried to extinguish his shoes against the wall of the TARDIS. 'I'm sure I keep a fire bucket handy somewhere...' the Doctor muttered, glancing around in an attempt to be helpful. But the shoes were already out, their blackened soles crumbling to ash in Rory's hands, so the Doctor simply shrugged and forgot about it.

He strode over to the railing along the gantry and leaned over to grin at his companions from their position by the door. 'It's called a thingy by the way,' he said.

'What is?' Amy asked.

'The thingy that delayed your mower's disintegration so that you could get here. I call it a thingy because I'm always forgetting the names of stuff, you see – I'm always going, "Where's that thingy?" and "What have I done with my thingy?" and "Ooh, what's my thingy doing there?" Now I'll always be looking for something specific, even if it isn't actually what I'm after.' He paused for a second and considered. 'Well, actually that could get quite annoying, especially if people kept passing it to me when I didn't need it.'

'I'd rather you'd not used a "thingy" at all, Doctor,' Rory began. 'I'd rather you'd just landed in front of us or something, you know, *before* the whole nuke thing.'

The Doctor shrugged and held up his palms. 'Sorry, couldn't move from the square, you see? It was the bomb's impact site and I couldn't deviate from those specific coordinates whilst carrying out my clever plan.'

'Which was?'

The Doctor hopped down the steps until he was standing in front of the pair. 'Saving my two best friends from dying in a nuclear explosion that had no place occuring in 1981, that's what.' He opened his arms and hugged them both tightly to his chest. 'Oh, and I got a new bike as well,' he said, pointing at the rusting contraption by the door.

Amy hesitated and pulled away from the hug. 'But it *did* go off, Doctor.'

'Sort of,' the Doctor replied, wondering how to explain what had just happened. 'It's like throwing something out of a moving car, a bit of rubbish or whatever. The TARDIS is like the car, the bomb is like the bit of rubbish, and the road outside is time, more importantly the time spanning one particular point so that driving forwards goes into the future of that point and reversing travels into the past, see?'

They didn't.

'If the car wasn't moving and you threw something out of the window, it would just hit the verge next to you. But if the car's moving really fast then the bit of rubbish will travel with the momentum of the car after it's thrown, hopping and skipping along the road behind it. I materialised the TARDIS around the nuke and took a run-up, ejecting it at the moment of impact. Because it was still moving rapidly forwards through time, the bomb's instantaneous explosion was spread over an hour and a half as it hopped and skipped across the future before coming to rest in normal time. The result was that the time line *knew* that a nuclear bomb was supposed to explode but was unsure *when*, so it took a while to catch up. In the end, to cover its tracks, it produced all the after-effects and destruction of a nuclear bomb, but combined it with a patchy and inconsistent moment of detonation. There's no mushroom cloud because there's no specific point for a mushroom cloud to occur, and you two have enough time to find me before the future catches on; especially as a pair of time anomalies like you are the last thing an uncertain past is going to try and impose consequences on.'

'Uh, right,' Rory mumbled. 'Well, thanks anyway.'

'You're welcome!' the Doctor replied cheerily, sauntering back up the steps to pack his flip chart away. 'Righty-ho, always moving on, moving on.'

Amy caught up with him before he could disappear down a corridor. 'That's it?' she said. 'That's all that happened to you – the run-up and the throwing-a-bomb-out-the-window thing – that was *everything*, was it?'

The Doctor shrugged. 'What do you mean?'

'I mean Albert. He didn't die. We remember him dying, we watched it happen. But he didn't die, Doctor, it never happened.' She frowned.

The Doctor looked away. 'Well isn't that nice for everyone?' he said.

'Isley said she saw you talking to him, at the military base.'

'You *spoke* to Isley?' The Doctor raised an eyebrow. 'If I'd known you were going to *make friends* with the killer androids, I'd have taken my time a bit more.'

'Be serious, Doctor.' Amy touched his shoulder, but he brushed it away.

'Today was a very long day, Amy,' he said eventually. 'I'm too tired for this.'

He turned and began to make his way down the corridor, boots clumping on the floor. Amy stood in silence for a second before resolving herself. She turned to see Rory waiting for her by the edge of the stairs and blew him a kiss. He caught it and stuck it on his bum with a wink.

Suddenly she turned back.

'Doctor!' she called after the retreating figure. He stopped. 'Did you do it, though? Did you manage to save them?'

The Doctor looked around and flashed his companion a sad smile. 'Yes,' he said quietly. 'Saved all of them. Every, single, one.'

And Amy was happy.

Chapter
19

Colorado, 28 August 1981, 5.20 p.m.

Albert pulled on a pair of goggles. 'I'm going outside,' he said simply.

A gantry had been erected along the exterior of the structure, running parallel to the observation room, and the wind tugged at his lab coat as he stepped onto the steel deck. It was like nothing he had ever seen before. The horizon sparkled in the distance, flashes of bright, blinding light flaring and dying amongst a flat sea of crimson flame. The display had lasted over ten minutes now and reminded the scientist of a lighthouse off the coast of a beach he'd used to holiday on as a child.

Inside the compound there was an awed silence,

rows of soldiers ranked up across the gates to the courtyard, taking it in turns to borrow the limited supply of goggles whilst the others turned their backs to avoid being blinded.

Albert's life was in that town, and it was burning.

'The Russian plane passed overhead three minutes ago.' Geoff was suddenly at his side. 'God knows what they'll make of this. God knows what *anyone* will make of this, it's like no nuke I've ever seen before.'

'Maybe that's a good thing,' Albert responded. 'More room to manoeuvre politically with an indescribable event.' For the first time in nearly ten years, he felt a glimmer of hope. 'It's up to Washington to make the right decision now.'

'Well we were all pretty freaked out when it came to crunch time. Even the boys in suits must have a heart somewhere.'

'No one wants to die,' Albert responded.

There was silence for a moment. Then Geoff coughed awkwardly.

'Albert, I think you should take a look at this.'

Albert was surprised to find Geoff's blue folder thrust into his hands. He looked up enquiringly.

'Just go through the summaries. It'll give you the gist.' Geoff nodded to him.

Carefully, Albert opened the folder, holding it

with his thumb to keep the papers from blowing away. The turning of sheets marked each passing minute until finally he handed the bundle back.

'It's not a huge surprise,' he said eventually. 'We've always been pretty dangerous – the things we know.' There was a pause. 'Do *they* know that you know?'

'No. A friend at the Pentagon passed it to me. These are the briefings they gave the platoon yesterday.'

Albert stepped back from the railing, out of sight of the soldiers below. 'So they've been ordered to shoot us?'

'Disappear is the preferred term. Who knows, they might actually let us live, in some form or other.'

'I think that depends on what you count as living,' Albert remarked.

Geoff coughed once more. 'But it's OK for you,' he said, 'because I got you this.' From behind his back he produced a parcel, brown Christmas wrapping paper tattered and torn at the edges. 'It took me a year. But I kept my promise.'

Albert gave him a look as he took the parcel, carefully tearing the edge off one side and shaking it a little before sliding his hand in to feel around.

He pulled out the items one by one.

The first was a little navy book.

'A passport – valid for anywhere,' said Geoff.

A wad of notes.

'One million dollars in traveller's cheques. That's my pension right there.' He smiled half-heartedly.

A small money bag, filled with dollars of varying denominations.

'Petty cash.'

And a key.

'There's a motorbike under a tarpaulin in the corner of the courtyard. It's yours.'

Albert had no words.

Geoff tried to laugh through his tears. 'There you go – a life, right there. The one we took away from you, the one *I* took away from you on that beach in California. All this –' he gestured at the horizon – 'is ended. Go and do what you always should have done.'

'But what about you?'

'I've had my life, before you. I had a wife and a kid, I had a house and a mortgage and a war. I don't think I could handle doing it all over again.'

Albert proffered his hand, and Geoff took it firmly.

'Thank you, old friend,' Albert said quietly.

'Oh, c'mere,' Geoff growled and embraced the scientist in a hug that almost lifted him off his feet. 'Now go, while they're still watching the show. If you can cross the state border before midnight it'll cause a hell of a fuss when they try coming after you tomorrow and you're long gone.'

Albert nodded. He shrugged off his grubby white lab coat and folded it neatly over the railing, then turned to walk down the steps.

Geoff waited for a moment before striding over to the top of the stairs. 'Just be happy,' he called after him.

Once Albert had disappeared around the bend, Colonel Geoffrey Redvers turned back to the horizon. He lifted his hands to his goggles and pulled them down to his neck, eyes squeezed tightly shut. He could feel the warm breeze from the horizon running across his face and hands, through his thinning grey hair. It felt pleasant and comforting like the arms of his wife, tight around his chest when he'd come home from the war.

'If I'm going to die tomorrow,' he said to himself, 'then I'll damn well enjoy today!'

A silent count of three, and he opened his eyes.

The highway was long and straight and empty as it ran through the desert towards the shadow of the mountain range in the far distance, and Albert pushed forward on the bike as he raced towards the sunset, the stones and rocks by the sides of the road blurring into a smooth golden brown. Geoff hadn't given him a helmet, and his tousled hair had flattened itself along his head, tugging at his face.

Even with his glasses on, he needed to squint against the wind to see where he was going, so he almost missed the figure walking slowly along the side of the road.

She was merely a dark shape at first, but her figure filled out as he approached and Albert could swear that he had seen that T-shirt somewhere before.

He braked gently as he drew alongside, the engine spluttering in frustration as he ground to a halt.

'Isley?'

The woman turned, and it was her. Her headphones had been wrapped together roughly in sticky tape – a bundle which also seemed to include a large chunk of her hair – and she had a scarf wrapped around half of her face.

'Albert, there you are,' she stated flatly. 'I was looking for you.'

'I'll bet you were,' Albert said, opening his arms and encouraging her to come closer. 'Come here. Let's take a look at you.'

She moved closer, and he reached out a hand to her scarf, tugging the material until it fell away.

Albert gasped.

Behind the scarf, the plastic skin of her face had melted away – a smooth line that ran from her right temple down to her lower jaw exposing the metal skull beneath. She held up her hand instinctively to cover the deformity, and Albert could see that it too had been stripped almost bare.

'I ran away from the village,' she said, 'but I wasn't quick enough.'

'No, I can see that,' Albert murmured. He ran the back of his finger softly across her smooth metal cheek and up to the speakers that covered her ears. He pulled them away softly and nodded as he recognised the track on the album. 'But why did you run?'

'To find you,' she said quietly. 'I need you.'

Albert leant over and kissed her tenderly. 'I need you, too,' he whispered. He composed himself and slapped a palm against the back seat of the motorcycle.

'Hop on then,' he said. 'We've got at least half an hour before you need to change the tape, and I want to be in New Mexico before nightfall.'

Acknowledgements

This book (and my career) would not exist if it weren't for Clayton Hickman and Gary Russell. It wouldn't look this good if it weren't for Lee Binding, and it wouldn't read this good if it weren't for the patience of Justin Richards and Steve Tribe.

Thanks also to Paul Lang, Claire Lister and Leanne Gill for giving me enough work to pay the rent whilst I wrote it, and Emma Price for paying it when they didn't.

Special mention must also go to all the wonderful people I've met since becoming part of the 'Whoniverse': Joe Lidster, Stuart Manning, Scott Handcock, Tom Spilsbury, Gareth Roberts, Darren Scott, Kieron Grant, Neil Corry, David Jorgensen and David Llwellyn, amongst many others.

I would also like to thank my family for stoically attempting to read all of my work, Thomas Coates Welsh for being a fellow *Who* fan and best mate throughout my childhood, and Tim Keable, who does the same today.

And finally, of course, Steven Moffat, Matt Smith, Karen Gillan and Arthur Darvill for crafting such a magical fairy tale.

DOCTOR █ WHO
Apollo 23
by Justin Richards

£6.99 ISBN 978 1 846 07200 0

An astronaut in full spacesuit appears out of thin air in a busy shopping centre. Maybe it's a publicity stunt.

A photo shows a well-dressed woman in a red coat lying dead at the edge of a crater on the dark side of the moon – beside her beloved dog 'Poochie'. Maybe it's a hoax.

But, as the Doctor and Amy find out, these are just minor events in a sinister plan to take over every human being on Earth. The plot centres on a secret military base on the moon – that's where Amy and the TARDIS are.

The Doctor is back on Earth, and without the TARDIS there's no way he can get to the moon to save Amy and defeat the aliens.

Or is there? The Doctor discovers one last great secret that could save humanity: Apollo 23.

A thrilling, all-new adventure featuring the Doctor and Amy, as played by Matt Smith and Karen Gillan in the spectacular hit series from BBC Television.

Available now from BBC Books:

DOCTOR WHO
The Forgotten Army
by Brian Minchin

£6.99 ISBN 978 1 846 07987 0

New York – one of the greatest cities on 21st-century Earth... But what's going on in the Museum? And is that really a Woolly Mammoth rampaging down Broadway?

An ordinary day becomes a time of terror, as the Doctor and Amy meet a new and deadly enemy. The vicious Army of the Vykoid are armed to the teeth and determined to enslave the human race. Even though they're only seven centimetres high.

With the Vykoid army swarming across Manhattan and sealing it from the world with a powerful alien force field, Amy has just 24 hours to find the Doctor and save the city. If she doesn't, the people of Manhattan will be taken to work in the doomed asteroid mines of the Vykoid home planet.

But as time starts to run out, who can she trust? And how far will she have to go to free New York from the Forgotten Army?

A thrilling, all-new adventure featuring the Doctor and Amy, as played by Matt Smith and Karen Gillan in the spectacular hit series from BBC Television.

Available now from BBC Books:

DOCTOR ⬛ WHO
The TARDIS Handbook
by Steve Tribe

£12.99 ISBN 978 1 846 07986 3

The inside scoop on 900 years of travel aboard the Doctor's famous time machine.

Everything you need to know about the TARDIS is here – where it came from, where it's been, how it works, and how it has changed since we first encountered it in that East London junkyard in 1963.

Including photographs, design drawings and concept artwork from different eras of the series, this handbook explores the ship's endless interior, looking inside its wardrobe and bedrooms, its power rooms and sick bay, its corridors and cloisters, and revealing just how the show's production teams have created the dimensionally transcendental police box, inside and out.

The TARDIS Handbook is the essential guide to the best ship in the universe.

Available now from BBC Books:

DOCTOR ⬚ WHO
The Glamour Chase
by Gary Russell

£6.99 ISBN 978 1 846 07988 7

An archaeological dig in 1936 unearths relics of another time... And – as the Doctor, Amy and Rory realise – another place. Another planet.

But if Enola Porter, noted adventuress, has really found evidence of an alien civilisation, how come she isn't famous? Why has Rory never heard of her? Added to that, since Amy's been travelling with him for a while now, why does she now think the Doctor is from Mars?

As the ancient spaceship reactivates, the Doctor discovers that nothing and no one can be trusted. The things that seem most real could actually be literal fabrications – and very deadly indeed.

Who can the Doctor believe when no one is what they seem? And how can he defeat an enemy who can bend matter itself to their will? For the Doctor, Amy and Rory – and all of humanity – the buried secrets of the past are very much a threat to the present...

A thrilling, all-new adventure featuring the Doctor, Amy and Rory, as played by Matt Smith, Karen Gillan and Arthur Darvill in the spectacular hit series from BBC Television.

Coming soon from BBC Books:

The Brilliant Book of

DOCTOR ⬚ WHO

Edited by Clayton Hickman

£12.99 ISBN 978 1 846 07991 7

Celebrate the rebirth of the UK's number one family drama series with this lavish hardback, containing everything you need to know about the Eleventh Doctor's first year.

Explore Amy Pond's home village, Leadworth, read a lost section from Churchill's memoirs that covers his adventures with the Doctor, and learn all about the legend of the Weeping Angels. See how the Doctor's costume evolved, how the monsters are made and discover the trade secrets of writing a thrilling *Doctor Who* script. Plus interviews with all of the key players and a few secret celebrity guests...

Including contributions from executive producer Steven Moffat, stars Matt Smith and Karen Gillan, and scriptwriters Mark Gatiss and Gareth Roberts, among others, and packed with beautiful original illustrations and never-before-seen pictures, *The Brilliant Book of Doctor Who* is the ultimate companion to the world's most successful science fiction series.